用LINE FB·IG 聊出好英文

只要**100**個
日常小話題，
英語能力
大跳級！

用 LINE
FB‧IG
聊出好英文

只要**100**個
日常小話題，
英語能力
大跳級！

Talk

Preface

前言

在路上一邊等紅綠燈一邊滑手機，「叮咚！」，這時來了一則訊息，嘴角浮起笑容，手指快速在手機上點著……觀察我們周圍，經常可以發現像這樣用手機和某人對話的場景。社群網路 (SNS, Social Networking Service，如 Facebook、LINE、IG 等) 已成為我們很熟悉的溝通工具，連結著每一個忙碌的現代人，從這點來看，社群網路將會是學習語言的一項利器，像我們這樣的 EFL (English as a Foreign Language, 以英文為外語的英語學習者) 可以從 SNS 獲得許多好處，基於此而有了本書的構想。

在教室裡透過老師與課本學到的英語和母語人士在實際生活中使用的英語，常讓學習者覺得有所不同，這或許可歸咎為整體學習環境的不良。現在就讓我們暫且把老師和學生之間的這種「透過課本學到的」尷尬英文拋開，來看看書中 9 位主角的日常生活故事，透過他們兄弟姊妹和朋友之間的「手機真實對話」讓讀者更有現實感，也能學習到目前流行的英文用法，為了引起讀者們的興趣，當然也免不了加了一點戲劇情節的元素 ^^~ 編寫本書時也考慮到國情與文化背景，讀者可按順序閱讀這 100 個小小的情境故事，或是隨意翻閱，找到「啊！就是這個！」的共鳴，期待讀者們最後把這些用法變成自己的語言。

最後要感謝長久以來給予編寫建議與交流機會的所有人士。

外師發音 MP3

請至碁峰網站：
http://books.gotop.com.tw/download/ALE003500 下載，存至電腦、手機或其他播放器聆聽，或是利用智慧手機等行動相關裝置掃瞄書中 QR Code 直接聆聽。內容僅供合法持有本書的讀者使用，未經授權不得抄襲、轉載或任意散佈。

Chatter & Chitchat

由日常生活、商務等 8 大類別 (Chatter) 和 100 個素材 (Chitchat) 構成，內容包括了主角的有趣故事和各種聊天八卦。

Chatting & Talking

背景是彩色的手機傳送訊息畫面，讓主角的對話更有臨場感，特別是按照每個主角的人物設定與場景，利用各種彩色插圖幫助讀者更快了解內容、增添學習樂趣。另外 More to Talk 也補充了各種相關句子幫助延伸學習。

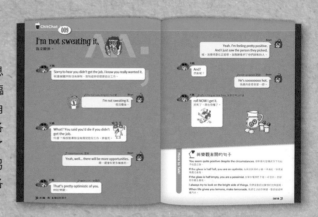

Review

按照類別與素材整理出學過的主要句子以便複習，也讓讀者能活用社群英語對話與實用會話。

Contents
目錄

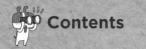 # Contents

Reference Charts
用英語聊天的參考資料

可按照情況選擇正式或非正式的用法。

１. 正式用法 v.s. 非正式用法

Formal	⟷	Informal
Good morning.	Hello. / Hi.	Hey.
Do you have time?	Are you busy?	U busy? / Busy?
Thank you.	Thanks.	Thanx / Thx
Could I call you later?	Can I call you later?	Call you later!
I'm looking forward to it.	Looking forward to it.	Can't wait!
Goodbye.	Bye.	Later.

２. 常用的聊天簡寫

lol, LOL	Laughing Out Loud	b/c	Because
lmao, LMAO	Laughing My Ass* Off	w/	With
rofl, ROFL	Rolling On the Floor Laughing	w/o	Without
U, u	You	XOXO	Hugs & Kisses
UR, ur	You're, Your	np	No Problem
R U, r u	Are you	Thx, Thanx	Thanks
Y	Why	TMI	Too Much Information
OIC, I C	Oh I See, I See	2nite	Tonight
OK, ok, K, k	Okay	2morro	Tomorrow
CU, See u	See you	GF	Girlfriend
OMG	Oh My God	BF	Boyfriend
OMF*G	Oh My F* God	BFF	Best Friend Forever
BTW	By The Way	ASAP	As Soon As Possible
Srsly?	Seriously?	SMH	Shaking My Head
NEway	Anyway	FYI	For Your Information
gtg, g2g	Got To Go	IMO	In My Opinion
BRB	Be Right Back	TY	Thank You
ttyl	Talk To You Later	W/B, wb	Write Back, 或是 Welcome Back
J/K, JK, jk	Just Kidding		

３. 常用的縮寫

Going + to = **gonna / gunna**	I'm gonna go tonight. U gonna go? / Gonna go?
Want + to = **wanna**	I wanna go out. U wanna..? / Wanna go out?
Got + to = **gotta**	I gotta go. / Gotta go.
Have + to = **hafta**	I hafta go. / Hafta clean my room.
Kind + of = **kinda**	I'm kinda busy. / Kinda busy.
Give + me = **gimmie**	Gimme a call later.
Don't + know = **dunno**	I dunno.
What + are+ you = **whatcha**	Whatcha doing?
Out + of = **outta**	I'm outta luck.

４. 英語聊天中常用的表情符號

笑臉	:)　　:o)　　=)
高興	:D　　:-D　　XD
眨眼	;)　　;-]　　;D
不高興	:/　　:-/　　>:\
傷心	:(　　:-[
生氣	>:(　　>:O
哭泣	:'(
伸舌頭	:P　　:-p　　XP
尷尬	:$　　:-$
不說話	:-X

Characters
登場人物介紹

安琪兒

個性溫柔的家庭主婦,是 Kell2013 的閨密,完全沒有工作經驗。

Kell2013

個性獨立的小資女、工作狂。常和朋友線上線下聊八卦來消除壓力。

小秘書

個性非常實際、勤快的法律事務所秘書,喜歡把自己從頭到腳打扮得漂漂亮亮。

電玩宅

個性很有趣的無業遊民兼電腦遊戲狂熱者,朋友認為他無法區分現實與假想世界。

天鵝

喜愛購物、時尚與流行音樂,夢想在時尚雜誌社工作,目前與多位男性交往中。

Bean

愛嘲諷,但其實是個性有趣的咖啡上癮女,對於無意義的約會感到疲倦的她最近引起了上司的莫名關心…

Jas

新創的遊戲公司社長,對工作有熱情又不焦躁,個性開朗,經常出差。

King_Michael

家庭背景雄厚,名校 MBA 學生。人生專注在商業、金融理財,是熱愛數位產品的 Early Adopter。

Tae

上班族,喜歡足球、籃球、棒球的美國人,單身,喜歡旅行。

CHAT

01

Work & Career
工作與職業

It's now or never. 機不可失。

 小秘書

I'm taking the afternoon off.
我下午會早點下班。

Kell2013

What's wrong?
有什麼事嗎？

 小秘書

♪ grad school: 研究所

I have a grad school interview.
我有一個研究所面試。

Kell2013

What? You haven't told me anything about this.
什麼？妳沒有告訴我有關這件事。

 小秘書

♪ chew ~ over: 仔細思考

I've been chewing this issue over since I don't know when.
不知從什麼時候開始，我就一直在考慮這件事。

Kell2013

...

小秘書

♪ have a feeling ~: 覺得 ~，有預感 ~

I have a feeling this is a dead-end job for me.
我覺得這是個沒有前途的工作。

Kell2013

I see. But you said you liked working there...
原來如此。可是妳說妳喜歡在那裡工作…

小秘書

I do. But time waits for no one.
沒錯，但是時間不等人。

Kell2013

But still...
不過還是…

小秘書

It's now or never.
機會稍縱即逝。

Kell2013

Well, good luck then.
那麼祝好運。

More to Talk!

 與支持、加油有關的句子

Which team are you rooting for? 你支持哪一隊？

Hope all goes well. 希望一切順利。

I'll always be there for you. 我總是在你身邊。

She has a supportive family. 她有支持她的家人。

He became financially independent right after graduation. 他畢業後馬上就經濟獨立了。

I can feel it in my bones! 我有預感！

 Bean

I need a favor. Can I borrow your blue blazer?
我有一個請求，我可以借妳的藍色西裝外套嗎？

 天鵝

Of course. You have good timing!
Just picked it up from the cleaner's. lol
當然，妳時間選得正好！我剛從洗衣店拿回來。

 Bean

Awesome! Thank you!!! I'll stop by tonight to pick it up.
太棒了！謝謝妳！我今晚會順便去拿。

 天鵝

Cool. What's the occasion?
好，是什麼場合呢？

 Bean

I've got an interview. They're looking for
a new assistant manager at work.
我有一個面試，他們公司正在找一位新的副理。

 天鵝

I'm sure you'll get it. You are the star employee after all. ;)
我相信妳可以的，妳畢竟是明星職員 :)

 Bean

Oh, I'm going to get it. I can feel it in my bones.
嗯，我會的，我有預感！

 天鵝

Confident much?
很有自信呢？

Bean

You know it! I've been there only two years and have been employee of the month like 9 times already.

妳知道的，我只在這裡 2 年就已經拿到 9 次當月模範員工了。

天鵝

lol
呵呵。

Bean

Not only that but I know the hiring manager.
She's super nice and told me to apply for the position herself.

不只這樣，我還認識人事經理，她人非常好，告訴我可應徵這個職位。

🖉Not that you'll need it.: (不特別懇切期望，因為確信將會順利) 雖然你不需要。　天鵝

Nice. Well, good luck. Not that you'll need it.

很好啊，祝妳好運，雖然妳不需要。

Bean 　　🖉Thx: Thanks 的網路簡寫

Haha thx. Gotta go though. I'll give you a call tonight when I get out of work.

哈哈，謝謝。我得走了，今晚下班後會打電話給妳。

🖉K: OK 的網路簡寫　天鵝

K. See you later.
OK，待會見。

 ## 與自信有關的句子

Don't worry, I've got this! 不要擔心，我會看著辦的。

Piece of cake! 太簡單了！

I am in total control of the situation. 我可以完全掌握狀況。

I have no doubt in my mind. 我一點也不懷疑。

I'm a perfect fit! 我就是不二人選！

You've got what they want.

你有他們想要的。

 Kell2013

Coffee tomorrow?
明天要喝咖啡嗎？

 Jas

🖉go on a biz trip: 出差 / biz: business 的簡寫

Sorry. I'm going on a biz trip.
抱歉，我明天要出差。

 Kell2013

Again? Where to?
又要？去哪裡？

Jas

Singapore.
新加坡。

 Kell2013

🖉most of the time: 大部份、幾乎所有時間

It seems like you're out of the country most of time.
你似乎大部份時間都在國外。

 Jas

🖉attract investors: 吸引投資者

I need to attract more foreign investors.
我需要吸引更多外國投資者。

Kell2013   🔖Don't worry about a thing: 不用擔心，一點也不用擔心

Don't worry about a thing. They'll definitely want to invest.
別擔心，他們一定想投資的。

🔖Thanx: Thanks 的簡寫   Jas

Thanx.
謝謝。

Kell2013   🔖You've got what they want: 你有他們想要的，你就是適合的人。

I'm telling you. You've got what they want.
我是說真的，你有他們想要的。

🔖pep talk: 鼓勵的話   Jas

Thanks for the pep talk. :)
謝謝妳的鼓勵。

Kell2013   🔖Anytime/any time: 隨時 / 不用客氣

Anytime. :D
不用客氣。 :D

🔖You just made my day: 你讓我心情很好。   Jas

No, really. You just made my day! :)
不，真的，妳讓我心情很好。

More to Talk!

💡 與鼓勵、安慰有關的句子

Thank you for your encouragement. 謝謝你的鼓勵。
I was moved by his honest words. 我被他坦率的話感動了。
I feel much better after seeing you. 見到你之後，我覺得好多了。
Tell me something comforting. 跟我說一些安慰的話。
Don't try to sweet-talk me. 不要對我花言巧語。
I'm flattered. 太過獎了。

This project is my baby.

這個案子是我的寶貝。

 安琪兒

*work from paycheck to paycheck: 今天賺的今天花光

How's freelancing these days?
Still working paycheck to paycheck?
最近接案子接得如何？還是「月光族」嗎？

*at the moment: 就是現在，這瞬間　　　　　　　　Kell2013

Things are going great. Got a couple projects at the moment.
一切正進行得順利，現在有兩三個案子。

 安琪兒

Good to hear!
太好了！

*n: and 的簡寫　　　　　　　　Kell2013

Yeah n they all pay pretty well... except one.
嗯，而且報酬也相當好…除了一個案子。

 安琪兒　　　　　*take on: 承擔

So why even take it on? Time is money and
you can't afford to waste yours!
那妳為何要承接？ 時間就是金錢，妳不能浪費掉！

*potential: 有潛力的　　　　　　　　Kell2013

This is different. It doesn't pay much but it's got potential.
這個不一樣，雖然報酬不多，但很有潛力。

 安琪兒

Oh? Do tell.
喔？說說看。

♪All I can say is...: 我只能說　　　　　　　　　　　Kell2013

All I can say is that it's super exciting.
我只能說它超級令人興奮的。

安琪兒

♪tease: 捉弄、逗弄

...you're just going to tease me like that?
…妳這樣是在逗我嗎？

♪blow you away: 讓你驚訝　　　　　　　　　　　Kell2013

Sorry. I signed a confidentiality agreement. :/ But in a few months you'll find out. It's going to blow you away!
對不起，我簽了保密協議，但幾個月後妳會知道的，妳會大吃一驚！

安琪兒

Wow! You sound really enthusiastic.
哇！妳聽起來真的很熱衷。

♪baby: 非常珍惜的　　　　　　　　　　　　　　Kell2013

Yeah! This project is my baby. I'm so excited!!!
嗯！這個案子是我的寶貝，我非常興奮！！

More to Talk!

與報酬有關的句子

The minimum wage in this city isn't high enough. 這個城市的最低工資不夠高。

The salary is lower at C Company but they don't require as much overtime. C 公司的薪水比較低，但他們不要求太多加班。

They give raises every year after doing a performance review. 他們會在每年進行績效評價後調薪。

The salespeople at that store are a little pushy because they make commission off what they sell. 這家店的員工有點緊迫盯人，因為他們可以得到銷售獎金。

After taxes and living expenses there isn't much money left for savings.
支付稅金和生活費之後，就沒有多少錢可儲蓄了。

I'm flat broke.
我身無分文。

 Tae

Are you still playing that game?
你還在玩那個遊戲嗎？

🔖raid: 突襲、奇襲 / sword: 刀劍 電玩宅

Yeah, I just need to finish this raid and get my epic sword
對，我只需要完成這次突襲，得到這把超棒的劍就可以。

 Tae

Why don't you log off and join me for a drink?
你要不要登出遊戲和我喝一杯？

🔖flat broke: 一文不名的，完全破產的 電玩宅

I can't. I'm flat broke.
不行，我沒錢。

 Tae 🔖get off your ass: 把你的屁股挪開、起來 (用於熟人)

Maybe you'd have more money if you got off your ass and found a job.
如果你起來找工作，也許你會賺到更多錢。

電玩宅

🎧 bux: bucks 的簡寫、(美) 元

> **I AM working! This sword is worth 500 bux!**
> 我正在工作！這把劍值 500 美元！

 Tae　🎧IRL: in real life 的網路簡寫，實際的

> **IRL?**
> 實際的嗎？

🎧leave me alone: 離我遠一點、不要打擾我　電玩宅

> **Yeah, so leave me alone while I work!**
> 對，所以不要打擾我工作。

 Tae　🎧looks like ~: (It) looks like 的簡寫，好像 ~ / Drinks are on you. 酒錢你買單

> **Looks like drinks are on you next time!**
> 聽起來你下次要買單！

 與打擾有關的句子

Am I disturbing you? 我打擾到你了嗎？

Don't disturb me. I have loads of work to do. 不要打擾我，我有很多工作要做。

I didn't mean to stand in the(your) way. 我不是故意要擋住 (你的) 路。

Don't let the weather get you down. 不要因為天氣讓你心情不好。

I'm on a diet. Hunger is distracting me from doing work. 我正在減肥，飢餓使我工作分心。

(左側直排) More to Talk!

Been there, done that.
都是過來人。

 天鵝　✎ u: you 的網路簡寫

U know what I just did?
妳知道我剛剛做了什麼？

小秘書

What?
什麼？

 天鵝　✎ post: 張貼、刊登

Posted my resume.
我刊登了履歷。

小秘書

Oh really?
喔，真的嗎？

 天鵝

It's soooo stressful!
壓力好 ~~~~~ 大！

Been there, done that: I have been there and done that.
✎ 我也有這樣過，都是過來人。　　　　小秘書

Been there, done that.
我也是過來人。

 天鵝

I'm so stressed out.
我壓力好大。

小秘書

What are the odds?
機率如何？

 天鵝　𝄞slim: 稀少的、苗條的 / fierce: 兇猛的、激烈的

Slim. Competition is fierce.
很小，競爭很激烈。

𝄞hands-on experience: 現場經驗　小秘書

But you've got loads of hands-on experience...
不過妳有很多現場經驗…

 天鵝　𝄞be tired of ~: 厭倦於 ~ / working part-time: 兼職工作

Maybe too much. I'm tired of working part-time.
也許太多了。我已經厭倦了兼職。

𝄞make it: 成功　小秘書

Hope you make it this time!
希望妳這次能成功！

More to Talk!

💡 與經驗有關的句子

Have you ever met anyone you met on-line in person? 你曾經見過網友嗎？
It was my first time on a blind date. 這是我第一次相親。
Now I've seen it all. 現在我什麼都看過了。
Money has never made man happy. 金錢從來不會使人快樂。
Don't let this happen again! 不要讓這種事再次發生！

I'm in over my head.
超過我的負荷。

Jas

bout: about 的簡寫

Things are finally slowing down at work! How bout you?
工作總算放慢步調了，妳呢？

小秘書

Lucky you. I barely have enough time to shower in the mornings...
你真幸運。我連早上洗澡的時間都勉強擠出…

Jas

junior staff: 屬下員工

I see they work their junior staff pretty hard!
我看他們很會使喚下屬！

I'll say: 那麼、的確如此

小秘書

I'll say! And they want me to take all these foreign language tests...
就是說嘛！而且他們想要我去考所有的外語測驗…

Jas

Huh? I thought once you got the job you wouldn't have to worry about that kind of stuff.
嗯？我以為一旦妳找到工作了，妳就不用擔心那類的事情。

check one's specs: 檢查某人的資格 / specs: specifications 的簡寫

小秘書

So did I. Times sure have changed. Even after being hired they constantly check your specs.
我也是。時代已經變了，即使已經錄取，他們也繼續檢查你的資格。

Jas

So it seems... How are you coping?
好像是這樣…妳要怎麼應對？

🔖 be good at ~: 擅長 ~ / keep up with ~: 跟上 ~

小秘書

Not well. Everyone here is really good at English, Chinese, and even Japanese! I can't keep up with them. I'm in over my head. :'(
不怎麼樣，這裡每個人的英文、中文、甚至日文都很棒！我跟不上他們，
這對我是不可能的 :'(

Jas
🔖 take classes: 上課

I started taking Chinese classes on the weekends.
Any interest in joining?
我開始每個周末都去上中文課，有興趣加入嗎？

小秘書

Lots... but I work weekends too.
想啊…但是我周末也要工作。

 與資格有關的句子

I'm thinking of volunteering abroad so I can beef up my resume.
我正在考慮去當海外志工，這樣可以充實我的履歷。

A minimum TOEIC test score of 700 is required in order to be considered for employment. TOEIC 至少要 700 分才有應徵機會。

His test scores are really high but in reality he is quite poor at English conversation. 他的測驗分數非常高，但其實他的英文會話很爛。

Academics are important but you also have to have a decent amount of experience in the field. 學業很重要，但是你也必須在這領域有適當的經驗。

They are interested in people who are constantly trying to better themselves through study and volunteering. 他們對透過學業和志工活動來持續拓展自己的人感到興趣。

More to Talk!

It's a foot in the door.
你已經跨出第一步了。

 天鵝

I heard the news about your interview with S Company! Congratulations!!!
我聽到你要去 S 公司面試的消息了！恭喜！！

♫ It's not that big a deal.: 這沒什麼　King_Michael

Oh. It's not that big a deal...
喔，這沒什麼。

 天鵝

Not that big a deal? This is huge! It's so hard to pass their initial tests!
沒什麼？這很厲害啊！要通過他們的第一關測驗很困難！

King_Michael

Yes, but it's still only an interview.
是的，但這只是個面試。

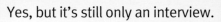

天鵝

It's a foot in the door.
你已經跨出第一步了。

King_Michael

Yeah... I guess.
嗯…算是吧！

 天鵝

You don't sound very excited.
你聽起來沒有很興奮。

It's just a lot of pressure. Plus my exams are coming. I'll be happy when all this is over with.
只是因為壓力很大而已，而且考試即將來臨，等到所有一切都結束我才高興得起來。

天鵝

🖊 I'll tell you what.: 我提個建議

Everything will be fine. I'll tell you what—if you pass the interview, I'll buy you dinner.
一切都會順利的。我看這樣好了，如果你通過面試，我就請你吃晚餐。

Just dinner?
只有晚餐嗎？

天鵝

Drinks too!
還有酒！

Sounds good to me. I'm going to go prepare for it now then.
聽起來很棒，那麼現在我要去準備了。

天鵝

Good luck!
祝好運！

與求職有關的句子

I've been to every recruiting agency in town; there just isn't any work out there! 我去過城裡的每一個求職中心，但那裡沒有任何工作機會！

There are several stages of interviews. 面試有幾個階段。

They get thousands of applicants everyday but hire very few.
他們每天收到幾千份應徵信，但雇用的人數很少。

I'm still waiting for a callback after my interview last month.
我仍然在等待上個月的面試回應。

More to Talk!

I'm not sweating it.

我沒關係。

天鵝

Sorry to hear you didn't get the job. I know you really wanted it.

很遺憾聽到妳沒有錄取，我知道妳很想要這份工作。

🖉I'm not sweating it.: 沒什麼　　　　　　　　Bean

I'm not sweating it.

我沒關係。

天鵝

What? You said you'd die if you didn't get the job.

什麼？妳說如果妳沒有得到這份工作，妳會死。

🖉opportunities: 機會　　　　　　　　　　　　Bean

Yeah, well... there will be more opportunities.

嗯…還會有更多機會的。

天鵝 🖉optimistic: 樂觀的

That's pretty optimistic of you.

妳好樂觀。

Bean

Yeah. I'm feeling pretty positive.
And I just saw the person they picked.
嗯，我覺得要往正面想。我剛剛看到了他們錄取的人。

天鵝

And?
然後呢？

🎵prob: problem 問題　　Bean

He's soooooooo hot.
他真的非常非常…帥。

天鵝　🎵rofl: rolling on the floor, 笑到在地上打滾

rofl NOW I get it.
笑死了，現在我懂了。

More to Talk!

 與樂觀有關的句子

You seem quite positive despite the circumstances. 你即使在這種狀況下也似乎相當正面。

If the glass is half full, you are an optimist. 如果你覺得杯子是一半滿的，你就是樂觀主義者。

If the glass is half empty, you are a pessimist. 如果你覺得杯子是一半空的，你就是悲觀主義者。

I always try to look on the bright side of things. 我總是嘗試往事情的光明面看。

When life gives you lemons, make lemonade. 如果生活給你檸檬，那就做成檸檬汽水。

YOLO (You Only Live Once)

活在當下。

Bean

> My colleague just got back to me about that internship we were talking about.
> 我同事剛回我有關我們剛剛在聊的實習工作。

天鵝

> Sweet! What did he say?
> 太棒了！他怎麼說？

Bean

> They are still looking for someone, but unfortunately it's unpaid.
> 他們還在找人，但可惜這個工作不支薪。

天鵝

> Oh... that's cool I guess.
> 喔…我想應該不錯吧！

Bean

> They at least pay for lunch and transportation costs. You should do it just to get your foot in the door.
> 至少他們會付午餐費和交通費。妳應該試試看邁出第一步。

天鵝

> Do they usually hire their interns?
> 他們常雇用實習生嗎？

Bean

🖉 networking opportunities: 獲得人脈的機會

> Only about 50%. But there are also lots of networking opportunities.
> 只有 50%，但這也是獲得許多人脈的機會。

✏️YOLO: (=You only live once) 你只能活一次。 天鵝

Hmm... okay! Why not? YOLO, right? lol
嗯…好！為何不試試？ YOLO，對吧？呵呵

Bean

Huh? What is YOLO?
嗯？什麼是 YOLO ？

天鵝

You don't know YOLO?
hahahaha It means you only live once!
妳不知道 YOLO ？哈哈哈，意思是活在當下！

Bean

Ahhh yeah I think I've heard that before.
啊 ~~ 嗯，我以前好像聽過。

✏️I bet ~: 我打賭 ~ / cray: crazy 的聊天用語 天鵝

I bet you don't know what cray is either.
我打賭妳也不知道什麼是 cray。

Bean

No idea. All I know is that you'd better not talk like that in the interview. lol
不知道。我只知道妳最好不要在面試上講這些，呵

 與人生有關的句子

Life's too short to sweat small stuff. 總是擔心小事，那人生就太短了。
Life's short; eat dessert first. 人生短暫，所以先吃甜點吧！
You only get one life so make the most of it. 你的人生只有一次，所以盡量利用吧！
Carpe diem! (Seize the day!) 享受當下！

It was a close call. 很驚險！

Kell2013

Didn't sleep a wink last night.
我昨晚一點也沒睡。

安琪兒

Why not?
為什麼？

Kell2013

🖉meet a deadline: 期限到了

I had a deadline to meet.
期限到了。

Dead line

安琪兒

Did you make it on time?
妳及時完成了嗎？

Kell2013

Of course.
當然。

Kell2013

🖉ruin one's reputation: 傷害名譽

Breaking deadlines would ruin my reputation as a freelancer.
超過期限會傷害我當自由工作者的名譽。

安琪兒

I agree.
沒錯。

Kell2013

🖉It was a close call: 很驚險、快被嚇死

Well, it was a close call.
這次很驚險。

🔖catch up on some sleep: 補眠　　　　安琪兒

Go home and catch up on some sleep.
回家去補點眠吧！

 Kell2013

I will. Thx.
我會的,謝謝。

🔖be about to ~: 正要 ~　　　　安琪兒

Actually, now you're about to harm your reputation.
其實,現在妳正在傷害妳的名譽。

 Kell2013

???

安琪兒

Don't you remember?
妳不記得了嗎?

安琪兒

We were supposed to meet 1 hour ago!!!
我們應該在一小時前就見面的!!

Kell2013　　　　🔖stick around: 原地不動

Ugh... Stick around. I'm on my way.
呃…妳不要動,我馬上去。

💡 與等待有關的句子

Stay where you are. I'll be there in a bit. 你在那裡等,我馬上到。

Stay put. I'm coming! 不要動,我馬上來!

Don't go anywhere. I'll be there in 10. 哪裡也別去,我 10 分鐘後到。

Wait a sec. I'll be right with you. 等 1 秒,我馬上到。

I'll be right over. I'm already there. 我馬上到,我已經快到了。

Working around the clock is a must to get ahead.

要成功就要 24 小時一直工作。

 小秘書

> Are you working late again?
> 妳又工作到很晚嗎？

 Kell2013

> Yeah, I have a deadline tomorrow afternoon.
> 對，期限到明天下午。

 小秘書　　🔖 be burn out: 體力耗盡、極度勞累

> Well, don't work too hard. You might burn yourself out!
> 嗯，工作不要太努力了，妳可能會累死！

🔖 work around the clock: 24 小時工作 / a must to get ahead: 成功的必要條件 Kell2013

> They say that working around the clock is a must to get ahead.
> 要成功就要 24 小時一直工作。

 小秘書

> Well, don't forget me when you get too far ahead!
> 那麼，當妳非常～成功時，別忘了我。

🎵BFF: best friend forever 永遠的好朋友　Kell2013

Lol. How can I forget my BF?!?
呵呵，我怎會忘了我的閨密？

小秘書 🎵little people: 小人物

Just don't forget the little people!
可別忘了小人物！

Kell2013

lol I'll buy you lunch every day!
呵呵，我會每天請妳吃午餐。

小秘書 🎵You better. =You'd better: 最好

You better. ;)
妳最好能做到 ;)

 與過勞有關的句子

Working too hard is bad for your health. 工作過度有損你的健康。

All work and no play makes you a boring person! 只工作不玩會讓你變成無趣的人。

The deadline's been extended so don't overwork yourself. 期限延期了，所以你不要過勞。

Her boss worked himself to death. 她的老闆因過勞過世了。

I owe you a big one.

我欠你一個人情。

 電玩宅

I heard you have a friend who owns a game company.
我聽說你有一個朋友在經營遊戲公司。

Tae

Yeah, Jas. He's a pretty cool guy. What's up?
對，是 Jas，他是很不錯的人。怎麼了？

 電玩宅

Do you know if he's hiring?
你知道他有在招人嗎？

Tae

Not sure, but I can ask him. Why?
我不確定，但我可以問他。怎麼了？

 電玩宅

You know how much I love to play games, and I thought it would be fun to work at a game company.
你知道我有多喜歡玩遊戲，我想在遊戲公司工作會很有趣。

🖋under stress: 承受壓力

Tae

Yeah, but I don't think it's all fun and games. Jas always seems to be under stress.
嗯，但我不認為這個工作總是有趣和只玩遊戲。Jas 似乎常常承受壓力。

電玩宅

You know what they say?
Nothing in life is easy.
你沒聽過這句話嗎？人生沒有容易的事。

♪ain't: 非標準用語，be 動詞 + not 的省略型　Tae

Ain't that the truth.
嗯，不變的真理。

電玩宅

Do you think you can introduce me to
Jas and maybe get me an interview?
你想你能把我介紹給 Jas，也許會讓我面試一下？

Tae

Sure, I'm supposed to have lunch with him this week.
I'll introduce you two.
當然，我想這星期會和他吃午餐，我會介紹你們兩個。

電玩宅　♪owe someone a big one: 欠某人一個大人情

Thanks, I owe you a big one.
謝謝，我欠你一個大人情。

 與壓力有關的句子

Too much stress can cause a sleep disorder. 過度的壓力會造成睡眠障礙。

I wanna know how to de-stress. 我想知道如何消除壓力。

How can I get rid of my stress? 我要如何消除壓力？

I just wanna work in a less stressful work environment. 我只想在壓力較小的
工作環境下工作。

Chronic stress affects your immune system. 慢性壓力會影響你的免疫系統。

I smell a rat.
我覺得事有蹊蹺。

Bean

🏷let ~ go: 讓 ~ 走，解雇

They let another person go today.
公司今天又解僱了一個人。

🏷severe: 殘酷的

安琪兒

You've got to be kidding me! Your new manager is so severe!
妳一定是在開玩笑！妳的新經理好嚴苛！

Bean

🏷You're telling me.: 我就說嘛！

You're telling me! He fired this one for not being "cheery" enough.
我就說嘛！他解雇這個人是因為他不夠「開朗」。

安琪兒

Dang.
該死。

Bean

🏷ppl: people 的簡寫，人們

Yeah. And this person is one of cheeriest ppl I know. Something is not right.
嗯，而且這個人是我認識的人之中最開朗的，事情不太對。

安琪兒

You think there is something else going on?
你覺得還會發生其他事嗎？

Bean

Well I heard that he used to manage another café in town that went out of business.
嗯，我聽說他曾經在市區內經營另一家咖啡店，那家已經倒閉了。

安琪兒

Oh?
哦？

Bean

Apparently he was really close with the staff there. Like family.
很明顯地他和那裡的員工非常親近，就像家人。

安琪兒

Uh-huh...
嗯…

Bean

Well most of them are still looking for jobs...
And our place just lost a bunch of staff!
他們大部份都還在找工作…而我們咖啡店剛解僱了一堆員工！

安琪兒

I smell a rat!
我覺得事有蹊蹺。

 與懷疑有關的句子

More to Talk!

Something fishy is going on at the office. 辦公室裡有些可疑的事情。

A lot of strange things have been going on. 太多奇怪的事情發生了。

Does he seem suspicious to you? 他似乎很可疑嗎？

I wouldn't tell her; I'm not sure she is trustworthy. 我不會告訴她，我不確定她是否值得信任。

ChitChat 001　　p 14

It's now or never.

take the afternoon of　只有早上工作
grad school　研究所
chew over ~　仔細思考
since I don't know when　不知是從何時
have a feeling ~　有預感 ~
dead-end job　沒有前途的工作
Time waits for no one.　時間不等人。
It's now or never.　機不可失。
root　支持
supportive　支持的
financially independent　經濟獨立

ChitChat 002　　p 16

I can feel it in my bones.

I need a favor.　我有一個請求。
the cleaner's　洗衣店
stop by　順便去
What's the occasion?　是什麼場合呢？
assistant manager　副理
I can feel it in my bones.　我有預感。
You know it!　你知道的！
employee of the month　當月模範員工
hiring manager　人事經理
Not that you'll need it.　雖然妳不需要。
get out of work　下班
piece of cake　太簡單了
have no doubt　一點也不懷疑
I'm a perfect fit.　我是不二人選。

ChitChat 003　　p 18

You've got what they want.

go on a biz trip　出差
most of time　大部份時間
attract investors　吸引投資者
Don't worry about a thing.　一點也不用擔心。
invest　投資
You've got what they want.　你有他們想要的。
pep talk　鼓勵的話語
You made my day.　妳讓我心情很好。
encouragement　鼓勵
move　感動
comforting　令人安慰的
sweet-talk someone　對 ~ 說甜言蜜語
I'm flattered.　過獎了。

ChitChat 004　　p 20

This project is my baby.

freelancing　自由接案
work paycheck to paycheck　月光族
Things are going great.　事情進行得順利。
take on　承擔
afford　可負擔的
potential　有潛力的
All I can say is...　我只能說…
tease　捉弄
confidentiality agreement　保密協定
in a few months　幾個月內

This project is my baby. 這個計畫是我的寶貝。

overtime 超時工作

performance review 績效評價

commission 手續費

ChitChat **005** p 22

I'm flat broke.

Join me for a drink. 和我一起喝一杯。

I'm flat broke. 我身無分文。

bux bucks (美) 元

in real life 現實生活中

Leave me alone. 離我遠一點。

Drinks are on me. 酒錢我買單。

ChitChat **006** p 24

Been there, done that.

post one's resume 刊登 ~ 的履歷

Been there, done that. 都是過來人。

stressed out 壓力很大

fierce 激烈的

hands-on experience 現場經驗

work part-time 兼職工作

make it 成功、完成

I've seen it all. 現在我什麼都看過了。

ChitChat **007** p 26

I'm in over my head.

slow down 速度放慢

Lucky you. 你真幸運。

junior staff 屬下員工

I'll say. 的確如此。

that kind of stuff 那類的事

I'm in over my head. 超過我的負荷。

take classes 上課

ChitChat **008** p 28

It's a foot in the door.

congratulation 恭喜

Congratulations. 恭喜。

It's not that big a deal. 沒什麼。

initial 初期的

It's a foot in the door. 妳已經跨出第一步了。

pressure 壓力

I'll tell you what. 我看這樣好了。

pass the interview 通過面試

preliminary 預備的

applicant 應徵者

callback 回應

ChitChat **009** p 30

I'm not sweating it.

I'm not sweating it. 我沒關係。

optimistic 樂觀的

positive 正面的
circumstances 狀況
optimist 樂觀主義者
pessimist 悲觀主義者
look on the bright side 往好的方面想

ChitChat **010** p 32

YOLO (You Only Live Once)

colleague 同事
transportation cost 交通費
hire 雇用
networking 累積人脈
YOLO (You Only Live Once) 活在當下
sweat 擔心
make the most of 盡量利用
Carpe diem! 享受當下！

ChitChat **011** p 34

It was a close call.

do (not) sleep a wink 一點也沒睡著
on time 及時
break deadlines 超過期限
ruin one's reputation 傷害名譽
reputation 名譽
freelancer 自由工作者
It was a close call 很驚險、快被嚇死
catch up on some sleep 補眠
harm one's reputation 傷害～的名譽
stick around 原地不動

ChitChat **012** p 36

Working around the clock is a must to get ahead.

burn oneself out 體力耗盡
Working around the clock is a must to get ahead. 要成功就要 24 小時一直工作。
BF 最好的朋友
little people 小人物
You better. 你最好能做到。
overwork 過勞
work to death 過勞死

ChitChat **013** p 38

I owe you a big one.

own 擁有
under stress 承受壓力
I owe you a big one. 我欠你一個人情。
sleep disorder 睡眠障礙
immune system 免疫系統

ChitChat **014** p 40

I smell a rat.

let someone go 解雇
severe 殘酷的、嚴苛的
go out of business 倒閉
staff 職員
I smell a rat. 我覺得事有蹊蹺。
fishy 可疑的
suspicious 奇怪的

CHAT

02

Appearance

外在

You should call ahead for an appointment.

你應該先打電話預約。

 小秘書

 小秘書

See this?
看到這個了嗎？

 天鵝

Nice! Newly done?
好漂亮！新做的嗎？

小秘書   ✍ squeeze ~ in: 擠出時間

Yup! They squeezed me in at the last minute.
嗯！他們在最後一刻為我擠出時間了。

  天鵝

They look flawless. I love it.
它們看起來很完美，我喜歡。

小秘書   ✍ affordable: 買得起的、實惠的

They do a fantastic job while keeping it affordable.
他們做得很棒，價格也實惠。

  天鵝

Maybe I should visit the place. Where is it again?
也許我應該去看看，妳說在哪裡？

 小秘書   ✍ fl: floor 的簡寫 / bldg.: 大樓的簡寫

 On the 1st fl of my office bldg.
我公司大樓的一樓。

🎵 while I'm at it: 順便 天鵝

While I'm at it, I'll get a pedicure, too.
我去的時候也順便做腳指甲好了。

小秘書

You should call ahead for an appointment.
妳應該先打電話預約。

天鵝

I. C. Well, how often do you get a pedi?
我知道了。妳多久做一次指甲？

小秘書

Maybe once or twice a month. I also do it myself.
一個月一兩次。我也會自己做。

小秘書

天鵝

But removing dead skin is really a pain.
可是去角質很痛。

True.
沒錯。

🎵 after a while: 過一會兒 天鵝

Plus it makes your back hurt after a while.
而且之後背也會很痛。

小秘書

🎵 plz: please 的簡稱 / w/u: with you

Um, let me tag along w/u. Make it for two plz.
嗯，讓我和妳一起去，請預約兩個人。

與預約有關的句子

I called to make a reservation. 我打電話預約了。

The shop takes walk-in customers too. 這家店也接受沒預約的客人。

I called two days ahead to get an appointment. 我前兩天打電話預約了。

They were fully booked so I couldn't get my nails done. 他們預約已滿，所以我不能做指甲。

Can I make a reservation for 2 at 5:00? 我能預約 5 點兩位嗎？

How about bangs?

剪瀏海如何？

 Kell2013

> Hey. Where r u?
> 嘿，妳在哪裡？

安琪兒

> At the hair salon.
> 我在美容院。

 Kell2013

> Getting a perm?
> 燙頭髮嗎？

安琪兒

> Nope. I got that done last week. Remember?
> 沒有，我上星期才燙，記得嗎？

 Kell2013

> Whoops! Now I remember.
> 啊！我想起來了。

 🖉 pick on: 挑剔、找碴　　**安琪兒**

> My husband is picking on me about my new hairdo. >:(
> 我先生挑剔我的新髮型 :(

Kell2013

Um, ur hair looked good in the pic.
嗯，照片裡妳的頭髮看起來不錯啊。

do the magic: 變魔術

安琪兒

Photo filter did the magic.;)
照片濾鏡會變魔術：）

Kell2013

Really?
真的嗎？

安琪兒

Really really. So what should I do to look younger?
真的真的，所以我要怎麼做才能看起來年輕一點？

Kell2013

How about bangs? It'll take 10 years off of you.
剪瀏海如何？這會讓妳看起來年輕 10 歲。

與美容有關的句子

I'd like to get my hair straightened. 我想要把頭髮燙直。

You need to trim your hair to keep it healthy. 妳需要修整妳的頭髮以維持髮質健康。

She had her long hair cut short after breaking up with her bf. 她和男朋友分手後剪了她的長頭髮。

It's hard to grow out of a bad haircut. 頭髮剪壞的話就很難長回來。

Shampoo residue can cause an itchy scalp. 洗髮精殘留物會導致頭皮癢。

I went a little too far…

我有點太過了…

 電玩宅

> Wanna grab a bite? I'm down the street from your place.
> 要吃點什麼嗎？我在妳家附近的街上。

Bean

> No. I'm never leaving this house again!
> 不要，我再也不要離開家了！

 電玩宅

> Lol why's that?
> 呵呵，為什麼那樣？

🔑It's a disaster.: 這是場災難，完蛋了　　　　　　Bean

> My hair. It's a disaster. I just got the worst haircut of my life.
> 我的頭髮，真是場災難。我剛剪了一個人生中最糟糕的髮型。

 電玩宅

> They cut it a little too short? I'm sure it's not that bad.
> 剪得太短了嗎？我想不會那麼糟。

Bean

> It's waaaay too short. And blonde. :X
> 太 ~~~~~ 短了，而且是金髮。

 電玩宅

> Blonde? You dyed it too?
> 金髮？妳也染髮了？

🎵main character: 主角 / copy one's style: 複製 ~ 的造型　　　　　Bean

> I was watching some American movie and the main character was so cute so I tried to copy her style.
> 我看了一些美國電影，主角非常可愛，所以我想嘗試她的造型。

Bean

> I went a little too far...
> 我有點太過了…

 電玩宅　　　　　　　　　　　　🎵throw on ~: 隨便套上

> There's not a thing you could do to make yourself look bad. How about throwing on a hat and meeting me?
> 妳怎麼樣也不會看起來很醜。隨便戴個帽子出來見我如何？

Bean

> You buying?
> 你請客？

 電玩宅　🎵You coming?: Are you coming? 的簡寫

> Yeah. You coming?
> 對，妳要來嗎？

Bean

> Sure, why not? XD
> 當然，為何不去？

💡 與美容有關的句子

I asked them to cut it shoulder length but look how short it is! 我要求他們剪到肩膀，但看看短成什麼樣子！

I ask them for a shampoo too because I love the way they massage my scalp. 我請他們幫我洗頭髮，因為我喜歡他們按摩我的頭皮。

I've been getting my hair permed for years. 我過去好幾年都燙頭髮。

Buying hair dye and coloring your hair at home is so much cheaper. 買染髮劑在家染髮會更便宜。

They also do eyebrow waxing and tanning there. 他們也有蜜蠟修眉、染眉。

I couldn't even recognize her!

我甚至認不出她了！

 天鵝

> **Bean! Guess who I met today.**
> Bean！猜猜看我今天遇到誰了。

 Bean

> **Who?**
> 誰？

 天鵝

> **Joohee from high school.**
> 高中同學 Joohee。

Bean

> **I haven't seen her in years. How is she?**
> 我好幾年沒見過她了，她還好嗎？

 天鵝

> **I couldn't even recognize her.**
> 我甚至認不出她了！

Bean

> **She looks that different???**
> 她看起來那麼不一樣嗎？

 天鵝

 lose weight: 減肥

> **She lost soooo much weight.**
> **She weighs half of what she did in HS.**
> 她瘦非常～多。比起高中時她瘦了一半。

 Bean

> **Really?**
> 真的？

天鵝　　　　　　　　　　　　🎧on top of that: 不只如此、而且

On top of that, she underwent multiple plastic surgeries.
而且她經過了很多次整形手術。

🎧speechless: 無話可說　　Bean

I'm speechless. :-X
我無話可說了。

 天鵝　🎧thing is: 問題是、其實

Thing is...
問題是…

Bean

???

 天鵝　🎧full of oneself: 自以為是、傲慢的

She seemed a little full of herself.
她似乎有點自以為是。

Bean

Oh, well...
喔…

More to Talk!

與美容有關的句子

She has had a lot of work done. 她做了很多次整形手術。
I felt refreshed after getting a massage. 接受按摩之後，我覺得很清爽。
Have you thought of getting a nose job? 妳想做隆鼻手術嗎？
His aunt got facial Botox injections. 他的嬸嬸在臉上注射了肉毒桿菌。
I'm going to get permanent eyeliner done. 我要紋眼線。

019

I can't get rid of this backne. 我無法擺脫這個痘痘。

Kell2013

🖉cuz of: because of 的簡寫

> Why'd you cancel on the Busan trip? 班喬 says it's cuz of work but I know that's not true.
> 妳為何取消了釜山旅行？班喬說是因為工作，但我不相信。

小秘書

> It's embarrassing.
> 因為很尷尬。

Kell2013　🖉spill: 說出

> I won't tell anyone. Spill.
> 我不會告訴任何人，說吧。

🖉bathing suit: 游泳衣　小秘書

> I don't want to wear a bathing suit.
> 我不想穿泳衣。

Kell2013　🖉self-conscious: 自我意識強的、意識到別人視線的

> Oh, don't be silly. We all feel self-conscious about our bodies. But you're the skinniest one of us!
> 喔，別傻了，我們都會對身體感到忸怩，但妳是我們之中最苗條的。

Kell2013　🖉bare: 裸體的、衣服破爛的

> If we can bare it all so can you!
> 如果我們都能脫光，妳也可以！

小秘書

It's not my weight. It's my skin.
不是因為我的體重,而是皮膚。

Kell2013　🔖immaculate: 完美無瑕的

Your skin is immaculate!
妳的皮膚很完美!

🔖backne: back+ acne, 背部和痘痘的合成詞　小秘書

Not my face... my body!
I can't get rid of this backne. :'(
不是臉…是我的身體!我無法擺脫這個痘痘 :(

Kell2013　🔖clear that up: 清除那個 / in no time: 馬上

That's all? Why didn't you just say so! I know a dermatologist that can clear that up in no time.
就只是那樣? 那妳就直說啊!我知道有個可以馬上弄乾淨的皮膚科醫生。

與皮膚有關的句子

My chin keeps breaking out! 我的下巴一直長東西。

My mom keeps her skin healthy by getting an exfoliating massage at the bath house. 我媽媽在公共澡池裡搓澡來管理她的皮膚。

There is a new cream on the market that is supposed to reduce age spots. 新上市的乳霜被認為可減少老人斑。

I'm thinking about getting a little work done on my face. 我想在我的臉上動一點手術。

Everyone likes a white complexion but I prefer darker skin. 每個人都喜歡白皮膚,但我比較偏好黝黑皮膚。

More to Talk!

You've got to look the part.
你必須看起來適合那裡。

 King_Michael

Nice profile pic.
大頭照很好看。

電玩宅

Thanks. Do I look like a professional or what? Lol
謝謝。我看起來像不像專業人士？呵呵。

 King_Michael

🖉n: and 的簡寫

I'm shocked to see you out of a t-shirt n sneakers.
我很驚訝看到你脫下 T 恤和運動鞋。

🖉suit: 一整套的西裝

電玩宅

Heh. But what do you think of the suit?
嘿，你覺得這套西裝如何？

 King_Michael 🖉top notch: 最棒的、一流的

Top notch.
非常棒！

🖉go well together: 很適合

電玩宅

And the tie? Do they go well together?
那這條領帶呢？它們有搭嗎？

King_Michael   🎵since when?: 何時開始？/ this stuff: 這類的東西

The whole ensemble looks great. Since when did you care so much about this stuff?
整體看起來都很棒，你何時開始關心這些東西的？

🎵get serious about: 對～認真   電玩宅

I decided it's time to get serious about getting a job. And if you want a good job you've got to look the part.
我決定這次要認真找工作了。如果你想要好工作，你就必須看來適合那裡。

King_Michael

Who are you?
你是誰啊？

🎵raid: 突襲、驚喜   電玩宅

Huh?
嗯？

King_Michael   🎵make the big money: 賺大錢

Nothing. So proud of you.
You'll be making the big money in no time.
沒什麼。為你驕傲，你馬上就會賺大錢了。

 與男性時尚有關的句子

I got my dad a pair of cufflinks for his birthday. 我送給爸爸一對袖扣當生日禮物。

They offer a shoe shining service as part of the hotel amenities. 他們提供的飯店服務之一是擦鞋。

An expensive watch can be considered an investment. 一支昂貴的手錶可被當成是一項投資。

After you buy the suit you have to get it tailored. 你買了西裝後，必須再量身剪裁。

He paired a corduroy blazer with jeans and it looked pretty good.
他搭配絨毛西裝外套和牛仔褲，看起來非常適合。

I have NOTHING to wear. 我沒有衣服可穿。

安琪兒

🎵 go to a wedding: 去結婚典禮

ARGH. This is so frustrating! I'm going to a wedding this weekend and I have NOTHING to wear.

啊～～這太令人沮喪了！我這周末要去參加結婚典禮，而我沒有衣服可穿。

🎵 filled to capacity: 滿滿的

Kell2013

What are you talking about? Your closet is filled to capacity.

妳在說什麼？妳的衣櫃裡有滿滿的衣服。

安琪兒

It's all last season's stuff. I need something new.

都是上一季的衣服了。我需要新的。

🎵 first birthday party: 周歲宴

Kell2013

What about that dress you wore to Haney's 1st birthday party?

妳上次穿去 Haney 的周歲宴那件如何？

安琪兒

I can't wear that again! Everyone has seen it!

我不能再穿一次！每個人都看過了！

Kell2013

That outfit you wore to brunch 2 weeks ago was also pretty cute.

兩個星期前妳去吃早午餐時穿的那件也很可愛。

安琪兒

stain: 弄髒

It's getting a little tight around the waist and the baby stained the blouse.

那件腰有點緊，而且寶寶把上衣弄髒了。

Kell2013

You know what this means?

妳知道這代表什麼？

安琪兒

Time to go shopping!!! :)

購物時間到了！！！

Are you in? 一起去吧？

Kell2013

Everything is on sale right now, too! Hehe Are you in?

而且現在每樣都在打折，嘿嘿，妳會去吧？

安琪兒

Yes, Ma'am!

是的，夫人！

與購物有關的句子

Everything in the store is on clearance. 店裡每樣東西都在大出清。

If you have a membership card you get a discount. 如果你有會員卡，你就能獲得折扣。

They won't let you try on anything before you buy it. 在你購買之前，他們不會讓你試穿。

The offer is buy one get one free so I got one for my cousin too.
這個是買一送一，所以我也給了表妹一個。

Their return policy is very strict so be careful about what you buy.
他們的退貨政策非常嚴格，所以買東西時要注意。

You look fresh off the runway. 妳好像在走伸展台。

 天鵝

Check me out!
看看我！

🔖fresh off the runway: 從伸展台上走出來　　小秘書

Gorgeous! You look fresh off the runway!
好漂亮！妳看起來好像在走伸展台！

Bean

Oooh! Where'd you get that dress?
哇～這件洋裝妳在哪裡買的？

 天鵝

🔖b/c: because / for a while: 短暫期間

Heh heh. It's cute right? It'd better be.
I'll be paying off my credit card for a while b/c of it.
嘿嘿，很漂亮對吧？一定得漂亮，因為它，我暫時用光了信用卡的額度。

🔖Oh, no: 喔，不、怎麼辦　　小秘書

Oh no. Did you really charge it?
You had finally paid down your old debt.
喔，不！妳真的刷了嗎？妳才終於還清了妳的舊債。

天鵝

📝 deserve: 值得、有 ~ 的資格

Don't be a nag! lol I deserve nice things. :P
It's a present to myself for getting an internship.
不要嘮叨了！呵呵，我也是可以買一些好東西的（吐舌頭）。
這是給我自己找到實習工作的禮物。

📝 work hard to (get a position): (為了獲得位置) 努力

小秘書

Well then good for you.
You did work really hard to get that position.
妳做得好。妳真的很努力工作才得到那個位置。

Bean

And now she can start working harder to pay off that debt. :P
而且她會開始更努力工作來還債（吐舌頭）。

小秘書

lollll
呵呵呵

天鵝

Forget you guys!
夠囉妳們！

More to Talk!

🛋 對自己好一點

I worked hard and now I want to reward myself. 我努力工作，現在我想要獎勵自己了。

It's important to take care of the kids but don't forget to take care of yourself. 照顧孩子很重要，但也別忘了照顧妳自己。

I'm going to spoil myself with a spa package. 我要用 spa 課程寵愛自己。

Let's treat ourselves to a night on the town. 讓我們去市區玩一個晚上！

Devote a day to pampering yourself at least once a month. 至少一個月一天對自己好一點。

Isn't it too showy for the first date?
第一次約會，會不會太誇張了？

 小秘書

> **Help me out!**
> 幫幫我！

安琪兒

> **?**

 小秘書

> **Check this out.**
> 看一下這個。

 小秘書

安琪兒

> **It looks WOW!**
> 看起來很棒！

 closet: 衣櫃

 小秘書

> **I searched through my closet all day to find it.**
> 我一整天翻遍了衣櫃才找到它。

安琪兒

> **Haha. So, who's the lucky guy?**
> 哈哈，所以誰是這個幸運的傢伙？

 小秘書

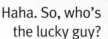 go out with ~: 和 ~ 約會 / tonite: tonight 的簡寫

> **Hyun. I'm going out with him tonite.**
> Hyun。今天晚上我要和他約會。

安琪兒

> **Hyun? Hyun, the hot lawyer????**
> Hyun？Hyun，那個性感的律師？

小秘書

Correct.
沒錯。

安琪兒

Awesome!!!
大棒了！！

小秘書

So, how do you like it?
所以妳覺得如何？

安琪兒

Nice.
很好。

小秘書

✎showy: 招搖的、誇張的

Uhmm... isn't it too showy
for the 1st date?
嗯…第一次約會，會不會太誇張了？

安琪兒

Personally I don't think it's too much.
我個人認為不會。

小秘書

✎get a 2nd opinion: 得到第 2 意見

Maybe I should get a 2nd opinion.
也許我應該尋求第 2 意見。

More to Talk!

 與衣服有關的句子

Guys like to show off their well-toned muscles by wearing tight clothes.
男生喜歡穿緊身衣來炫耀他們發達的肌肉。

After the 3-day crash diet, she's ready to wear something skimpy.
經過 3 天速成減肥，她準備好穿上暴露的衣服。

Thick makeup doesn't go well with her clean-cut outfit. 濃妝不適合她端莊
的衣裳。

Let me give you one important tip for appropriate business attire.
關於適當的上班族服飾，讓我給你一個重要秘訣。

I felt like I was underdressed for the party. 我覺得好像在派對上穿得不得體。

I look like I just rolled out of bed.

我看起來好像剛起床。

Kell2013 　　　　🎵on one's way: 正在路上、馬上抵達

Put your shoes on! I'm on my way over.
穿上妳的鞋子！我正在路上。

🎵Wha: what 的意思、咦？　　天鵝

Wha? Seriously?
咦？真的嗎？

Kell2013

Yeah. I'm almost there. About 5 minutes away.
嗯，我快到了，再 5 分鐘。

天鵝

No! I have to take a shower! Come by later.
不行！我必須洗個澡！晚點再來。

Kell2013 　　　　🎵throw on: 趕快穿上、隨便套上

No can do. I've got plans later. Just throw something on.
不行，我等一下有約。隨便套上一件吧！

♫ not suitable for innocent eyes: (因為樣子邋遢) 被別人看到很尷尬　天鵝

> **It's just you that's coming, right? I'm not suitable for innocent eyes.**
> 只有妳來，對吧？我被別人看到會很尷尬。

Kell2013

> **瓊絲 is with me!**
> 我和瓊絲一起！

♫ rolled out of bed: 剛滾下床　天鵝

> **Are you kidding? I look like I just rolled out of bed. Gimme some time!**
> 妳在開玩笑嗎？我看起來像剛起床。給我點時間！

Kell2013

> **Alright then we'll stop by in 20.**
> 好吧，我們會在 20 分鐘後過來。

天鵝

> **K. See u in 20.**
> OK，20 分鐘後見。

More to Talk!

 有關準備的句子

I need to get changed before we go. 在我們出發之前，我需要換衣服。

Do these shoes match my outfit? 這雙鞋子適合我的衣服嗎？

I have the perfect earrings to go with that necklace. 我有與那條項鍊搭配的完美耳環。

I pulled this outfit together in five minutes. 5 分鐘之內我穿好了這件衣服。

Can you help me pick something to wear? 你能幫我挑衣服穿嗎？

What's your point?

你的重點是什麼？

Beggars can't be choosers

安琪兒

What's your ideal type of guy?
你的理想型是哪種？

Kell2013

Oh dear. Why are you asking again?
喔，親愛的，為什麼妳又再問一次？

 安琪兒

Tell me!
告訴我！

Kell2013

Beggars can't be choosers...
我沒有挑人的資格…

 安琪兒

ROFL You're really not going to share?
快笑死，妳真的不要說嗎？

♪What's your point?: 妳的重點是什麼？　　Kell2013

Seriously, what's your point?
說真的，妳的重點是什麼？

 安琪兒

I'm looking for someone to set you up with.
我正在尋找介紹給妳的人。

Kell2013

Uhmmm... If you say so.
嗯…如果妳這樣說的話…

安琪兒

So?
所以？

Kell2013

Tall, dark, well-built, nice butt...
高個子、黝黑、強壯的體格、性感的屁股…

安琪兒

Hehe. Would that be all? ;)
嘿嘿，這就是全部嗎？

Kell2013

Of course not. The list goes on. Irresistibly handsome with a cute smile that kills me... filthy rich...
當然不是，還沒完。不可抵擋的帥度和可殺死我的可愛微笑…超級富有…

安琪兒

Now I get why you're still single. :P
現在我知道妳為何還是單身了（吐舌頭）。

與外貌有關的句子

You look much younger than your age. 你看起來比你的年齡年輕許多。
He's over 40, but looks half his age. 他超過40歲了，但看起來只有他年齡的一半。
You always look neat and well-groomed. 你總是看起來乾淨又整齊。
He has very good taste in fashion. 他很有時尚感。
He's going bald in his mid-twenties. 他在 20 多歲時就禿頭了。

ChitChat 015   p 46
You should call ahead for an appointment.

squeeze someone in 擠出時間
at the last minute 最後一刻
flawless 完美的
affordable 買得起的、實惠的
while I'm at it 順便
You should call ahead to make an appointment. 妳應該先打電話預約。
get a pedi 做指甲
pedi(pedicure) 美甲
twice a month 一個月兩次
remove dead skin 去角質
dead skin 角質
pain 痛苦、麻煩
after a while 過一會兒
tag along 一起去
Make it for two. 預約兩人。
walk-in customers 沒預約的客人
fully booked 預約已滿

ChitChat 016   p 48
How about bangs?

hair salon 美容院
get a perm 燙頭髮
pick on ~ 挑剔、找碴
hairdo 髮型
do the magic 變魔術
How about bangs? 剪瀏海如何？
bangs 瀏海

It'll take 10 years off of you. 這會讓妳看起來年輕 10 歲。
get one's hair straightened 燙直髮
trim one's hair 修整頭髮
itchy 癢的
scalp 頭皮

ChitChat 017   p 50
I went a little too far…

grab a bite 吃點東西
blond 金髮
dye 染色
main character 主角
copy one's style 複製 ~ 的造型
I went a little too far. 我有點太過了…
There's not a thing you could do. 妳無能為力。
throw on 隨便套上
shoulder length 齊肩
massage one's scalp 按摩頭皮
for years 幾年間
color one's hair 染色

ChitChat 018   p 52
I couldn't even recognize her!

recognize 認出
I couldn't even recognize her. 我甚至認不出她了！
lose weight 減肥
on top of that 不只如此
multiple 多次的
plastic surgery 整形手術

undergo a plastic surgery 做整型手術

I'm speechless. 我無話可說。

thing is... 問題是…、其實…

full of oneself 自以為是的

have a work done 做整形手術

get a massage 接受按摩

get a nose job 接受隆鼻手術

get facial Botox injections 在臉上打肉毒桿菌

eyeliner 眼線

ChitChat 019 p 54

I can't get rid of this backne.

Spill. 吐露、說出。

bathing suit 泳衣

self-conscious 自我意識強的、意識到別人視線的

skinny 苗條的

immaculate 完美無瑕的

get rid of 消除

backne 背上的痘痘

I can't get rid of this backne. 我無法擺脫這個痘痘。

dermatologist 皮膚科醫生

clear something up 清潔 ~

in no time 馬上

get an exfoliating massage 搓澡

bath house 公共澡堂

on the market 上市

age spots 老人斑

complexion 膚色

ChitChat 020 p 56

You've got to look the part.

top notch 最棒的、一流的

go well 適合

get serious about ~ 對 ~ 認真

look the part 適合這個部份、位置

proud 驕傲的

make the big money 賺大錢

shoe shining service 擦鞋服務

ChitChat 021 p 58

I have NOTHING to wear.

go to a wedding 去結婚典禮

I have nothing to wear. 我沒有可穿的衣服。

filled to capacity 滿滿的

first birthday party 周歲宴

outfit 衣裳

stain 弄髒

Are you in? 你會一起去吧？

clearance 存貨大出清

get a discount 獲得折扣

return policy 退貨政策

ChitChat 022 p 60

You look fresh off the runway.

fresh off the runway 從伸展台上走出

It'd better be. 最好。

pay off 償還

for a while 暫時

debt 債

nag 嘮叨

Don't be a nag. 不要嘮叨。
deserve 值得、有 ~ 的資格
treat oneself 對自己好

ChitChat 023　　　　p 62

Isn't it too showy for the first date?

search through 翻遍
Who's the lucky guy? 誰是那個幸運的傢伙？
showy 誇張的
It's too much 太過了，太誇張
get a second opinion 得到第二意見
show off 炫耀
well-toned 發達的
crash diet 速成減肥
skimpy 暴露的
clean-cut 端莊的
attire 服裝、衣裳
underdressed 不得體、簡陋的

ChitChat 024　　　　p 64

I look like I just rolled out of bed.

on my way 正在路上
come by later 晚點再來
No can do. 不行
throw on 隨便套上
suitable 合適的
innocent 無辜的
not suitable for innocent eyes （因為樣子邋遢）被別人看到很尷尬。

I look like I just rolled out of bed. 我看起來像剛起床。
get changed 換衣服

ChitChat 025　　　　p 66

What's your point?

Beggars can't be choosers. 我沒有挑人的資格…
What's your point? 你的重點是什麼？
If you say so. 如果妳這樣說的話。
well-built 強健的體格
butt 屁股
The list goes on. 清單還在繼續。
irresistibly 不可抵擋地
look half one's age 看起來像年齡的一半、看起來非常年輕
well-groomed 整齊的
have a good taste 有很好的品味
go bald 變禿頭
in one's mid-twenties 20 多歲

CHAT

03

Love

愛情

Love is one thing and marriage is another. 愛情和婚姻是兩回事。

 Jas

sign up with ~: 加入

I signed up with a professional matchmaking agency.
我加入了一個專業的婚友社。

Kell2013

You did WHAT???
你說什麼？？？

 Jas

decent: 不錯的，正經的

I decided to get some professional help finding a decent girl.
我決定尋求一些專業協助我找到不錯的女生。

go for: 喜歡、選擇   Kell2013

I thought that's the last thing you'd go for?
我以為那不會是你的選項？

 Jas

I think it'll be more practical.
我想那會比較實際。

go out with ~: 和 ~ 約會   Kell2013

What about all the girls you went out with?
你以前約會的女生們如何呢？

Jas

✎A is one thing and B is another: A 和 B 是兩回事。

Love is one thing and marriage is another.
愛情和婚姻是兩回事。

✎calculating: 善於算計的   Kell2013

Sounds TOO calculating.
聽起來太 ~ 會算了。

Jas

I'm super busy with work and...
我工作超級忙碌,而且…

✎arrange: 安排   Kell2013

... and they keep arranging dates for you?
所以他們持續為你安排約會?

Jas

That's it. This way I can focus on my work.
沒錯,這樣我可以專注於工作。

✎win-win situation: 雙贏局面   Kell2013

So it's a win-win situation for you.
所以這對你來說是雙贏。

More to Talk!

💡 與異性約會有關的句子 1

I was on a blind date. 我相親了。

I'll ask him out tomorrow. 我明天會要求和他約會。

Would you prefer love marriage or arranged marriage? 你比較喜歡戀愛結婚還是相親結婚?

She'll break up with him. 她將和他分手。

She got back together with him after all. 她終究和他復合了。

It's not like I have a ring on my finger. 還不到套上戒指的程度。

Bean

> Who was that guy I just saw you with? :O
> 我剛看到和妳在一起的人是誰？

天鵝

> Can't talk! On a date!
> 不能說！約會中！

Bean

> Whaaaaaaaaaaaat?! What happened to King_ Michael? Isn't he your boyfriend anymore?
> 什麼？？那 King_Michael 怎麼辦？他不是妳的男朋友嗎？

天鵝

> :P
> 吐舌頭~

Bean

> I thought you two had something going on. Am I wrong?
> 我以為你們兩個之間有什麼，我錯了嗎？

天鵝

> We're just talking...
> 我們只是聊天…

Bean

More than talking!
不只是聊天！

天鵝

Yeah but it's not like I have a ring on my finger.
沒錯，但還不到把戒指套在我手指的程度。

Bean

I am so out of the loop!
We need to grab a coffee and
have some serious girl talk.
我覺得像個局外人！我們需要喝杯咖啡，認真來個女孩之間的聊天。

天鵝

Haha True. Gotta go! Call u later. ;)
哈哈，沒錯，必須的！等一下打電話給妳 ;)

More to Talk!

 ## 與異性約會有關的句子 2

You two seem pretty serious these days. 你們兩個最近看起來好像是認真的。

We are not exclusive; I'm seeing other guys. 我們沒有交往，我也與其他人見面。

I'm not ready to settle down with one girl. 我還沒準備好和一個女生穩定下來。

I'm a "one-woman" kind of guy. 我是那種「只和一個女生」交往的男生。

I'm looking for a serious, committed relationship. 我正在尋找一段認真、有承諾的關係。

She won't give me the time of day. 她從來不給我機會。

 電玩宅

Can I ask you something? I need your advice.
我可以問你一些事嗎？我需要你的建議。

Tae

Shoot.
說。

 電玩宅

It's Bean.
有關 Bean。

Tae

What about her?
她怎麼了？

 電玩宅

She won't give me the time of day.
她都不理我。

Tae

Wait a minute...
等一下…

 電玩宅

I've tried everything.
我試過所有方法了。

🖊have a crush on ~：被 ~ 煞到，迷戀 ~

Tae

Are you telling me that you have a crush on Bean ?!??!
你說你被 Bean 煞到了？

電玩宅

I thought you knew. I thought everyone knew.
我以為你知道。我以為每個人都知道了。

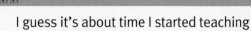
little brother: 弟弟   Tae

I guess it's about time I started teaching
my little brother about the ladies.
我想該是時候教一教我的弟弟有關女生的事。

電玩宅   _Don't patronize.: 少來這套_

Don't patronize. Just help.
少來這套了，只要幫忙就好。

Gimme a call tonite.: Give me a call tonight. 的口語，今晚打電話給我   Tae

Alright, alright. Gimmie a call tonite and we'll talk.
好吧，好吧，今晚打電話給我聊聊。

電玩宅   _Thanx: Thanks 的網路用語。_

Thanx!
謝啦！

 與異性約會有關的句子 3

I didn't know you had feelings for her! 我不知道你對她有感覺。

He is always going on about her, I think it's a crush. 他總是在談論她，我想這是愛慕吧！

My little sister has a thing for her tutor. 我妹妹喜歡她的家教老師。

I think they are more than just friends. 我想他們不只是普通朋友。

The two of them seem awfully close for just "friends". 他們兩個做為「朋友」似乎太過親暱了。

ChitChat 029

What's with you lately?

你最近怎麼了？

電玩宅

> **Where you been, bro?**
> 你去哪兒了？朋友？

King_Michael

> **Around...**
> 附近…

電玩宅

> **You never come out anymore.**
> **Haven't seen much of you online either.**
> 你都不出來，也不常在網路上看到你。

King_Michael

> **Just busy.**
> 就很忙。

電玩宅

> **You've never been too busy for just a drink.**
> **What's with you lately?**
> 你從來沒有忙到連喝一杯的時間都沒有。你最近怎麼了？

♪ return one's calls: 回電   King_Michael

> **I think 班喬 has moved on. She stopped returning my calls.**
> 我想班喬已經變心了，她不回我電話。

電玩宅

Maybe she's busy too?
也許她也很忙？

answer one's texts: 回訊息　　King_Michael

She won't answer my texts either.
She doesn't even check them.
她也不回我訊息，連看也不看。

電玩宅

Ah...
啊…

King_Michael

What do you think I should do?
你覺得我該怎麼做？

電玩宅

I guess you'd better forget her. Join me at the PC room?
我猜你最好忘了她，要不要和我去網咖？

King_Michael

...

More to Talk!

與分手徵兆有關的句子

You never respond to my messages! 你從來都不回我訊息！

Are you ignoring me? 你不理我嗎？

She hung up on me and turned off her phone. 她掛我的電話，還關機了

He barely even calls me anymore. 他現在連電話也不太打了。

I don't think he is interested in me. 我想他對我沒興趣。

Pull yourself together.

冷靜下來。

 小秘書

> **OMG! OMG! OMG!**
> 我的天啊！我的天啊！

Kell2013

> **What happened?**
> 怎麼了？

 小秘書　🖊make a mistake: 犯錯

> **I made a terrible mistake.**
> 我犯了個大錯。

Kell2013

> **What?**
> 什麼？

 小秘書　🖊be exclusive: 交往

> **I asked Hyun to be exclusive.**
> 我向 Hyun 提出交往。

🖊make the first move: 首先開始、首先採取行動　Kell2013

> **Wow! YOU made the first move!**
> 哇！妳先採取行動！

 小秘書　🖊go out of one's mind: 精神不正常

> **I must have gone out of my mind!!!**
> 我一定是精神不正常了！！

Kell2013

> **It doesn't always have to be the guy.**
> 並非一定要由男生提出。

小秘書

Oh, I can't even breathe!!!
喔，我甚至不能呼吸了！！

Kell2013

🔖pull oneself together: 收拾心情

Relax. Pull yourself together.
放輕鬆，冷靜下來。

小秘書

🔖regret -ing: 後悔

I'm already regretting asking him like that.
我已經後悔向他提出交往了。

Kell2013

Don't.
不要這樣。

小秘書

Yeah. I just did what I had to do.
好，我只是做了該做的事。

小秘書

🔖go on: 前進、繼續

I couldn't go on not telling him.
我不能不告訴他就這麼繼續下去。

Kell2013

Good. Good.
很好，很好。

 與後悔有關的句子

I shouldn't have said that. 我不應該那樣說。

Stop regretting your decision. 不要後悔妳的決定。

I feel really sorry for not seeing you one last time. 我覺得非常遺憾最後沒有看到你。

I'm terribly sorry for being careless. 我為我的輕率感到抱歉。

Regret over wasted time is more wasted time. 後悔浪費時間只是在浪費更多時間。

More to Talk!

It was a total disaster!

完全是個災難！

Kell2013　🔖 set A up with B 介紹 A 和 B 認識、安排相親

I heard 瓊絲 set you up with a girl.
我聽說瓊絲介紹了一個女生給你。

🔖 Yup: Yes 的口語　Jas

Yup.
嗯。

Kell2013

How'd it go?
後來如何了？

🔖 disaster: 災難　Jas

It was a total disaster.
完全是個災難！

Kell2013

Too bad.
太慘了。

🔖 talk my ear off that ~: 說 ~ 說到我耳朵長繭 / hot: 漂亮、性感的　Jas

瓊絲 talked my ear off saying that she was hot.
瓊絲說她很漂亮，說到我耳朵長繭。

Kell2013　🔖 ur: your 的網路簡寫 / r: are 的網路簡寫

Maybe ur standards r way too high.
也許你的標準太高了。

🔖 have a conversation with ~: 和 ~ 對話

Jas

I just want someone that I can have a nice conversation with.

我只想要一個好溝通的女生。

Kell2013

Ha!

哈！

🔖 reject: 拒絕 / hottie: 正妹

Jas

But who would reject a hottie?

不過誰會拒絕正妹呢？

Kell2013

🔖 shallow: 膚淺的

Ugh. How shallow!

噗！真膚淺！

與事情進展有關的句子

How's it going? 進行得如何了？

It was easier than I thought. 比我想的簡單。

We feel stuck with no way out. 我們覺得無法進展。

Well, the worst part is over. 嗯，最糟的部份已經結束了。

I'm sure we can make it one way or another. 我相信我們能找到成功的方法。

More to Talk!

Epic fail 史上最糟糕

 電玩宅

> I give up on women.
> 我放棄女生了。

 Tae

> lol Why's that?
> 呵呵，為什麼？

 電玩宅

> I just have no idea how to impress them.
> 我完全不知道要如何吸引她們。

 Tae

> Things didn't go well with Bean? Didn't you follow my advice?
> 和 Bean 不順利嗎？你沒照我的建議做嗎？

 電玩宅

> I made a fool of myself. I did like you said. I told her I was interested in what she's interested in.
> 我出醜了，我照你說的做，我告訴她她有興趣的事物，我也很有興趣。

 Tae

> Which is?
> 是什麼？

 電玩宅 🎵fancy-schmancy: fancy 和 schmancy 的音律相同而形成複合詞，意思是非常華麗

> Coffee. So I went to her café and ordered some fancy-schmancy drink. But the thing was so bitter I could barely drink it.
> 咖啡，所以我去她的咖啡店，點了一些非常花俏的飲料，但因為太苦我幾乎不敢喝。

🖊 SMH: shaking my head 的縮寫，表示搖頭的動作。

And she saw this? SMH...
所以她看到了？唉唉…

 電玩宅

Yeah I caught her looking at me. So I got really nervous and knocked the glass over. It shattered everywhere.
對，我看到她在看我，所以我非常緊張，把杯子打翻了，碎得到處都是。

Tae

Fail.
搞砸了。

 電玩宅

Then her boss came out screaming at her for having her friends wreck the place.
然後她老闆出來大罵她讓她的朋友毀了店裡。

Tae

Whoa... Epic fail. You're right to give up.lol
哇…史上最糟糕。你放棄得好，呵呵。

 與恥辱有關的句子

She probably thinks I'm a complete idiot. 她可能認為我是大白癡。

I'm not just embarrassed, I'm mortified! 我不只尷尬，還羞愧死了！

I can never show my face there again. 我再也不會去那裡露面了。

Can you believe he did that? What a clown! 你相信他做了那件事？太愚蠢了！

It was so humiliating. I never want to do it again! 這真是太羞恥了，我再也不會那樣做！

It's just not working.

行不通的。

 King_Michael 🎵answer one's messages: 回覆 ~ 的訊息

Why aren't you answering my messages?
妳為何不回覆我的訊息？

天鵝

Things are really crazy lately. Sorry.
最近完全忙瘋了，抱歉。

 King_Michael

It seems like you're not interested in me anymore.
妳似乎不再對我有興趣了。

天鵝

...

 King_Michael

You don't have anything to say?
妳沒有任何要說的嗎？

天鵝

We need to talk. Want to meet next weekend?
我們需要談談，要不要下週末見面？

King_Michael

Seriously? Next weekend? Don't you think that's a little late?
真的？下週末？妳不覺得太慢了嗎？

天鵝

Listen, Michael. It's just not working.
聽著，Michael，我們二個行不通的。

King_Michael

You're breaking up with me by text message?
妳要用簡訊和我分手？

天鵝

Sorry.
對不起。

King_Michael   📎whatever: 隨妳便

Whatever.
隨妳便。

 與分手有關的句子

More to Talk!

Can't we just start over? 我們不能重新開始嗎？
Just give me another chance. 再給我一次機會。
I'm still really into you. 我還是非常喜歡你。
We can't work it out. 我們行不通的。
I'm not going to give you up without a fight. 我不會輕易放棄你的。

Friendship between men and women is impossible. Period.

男女之間沒有純友誼，以上。

小秘書

> I need a guy's point of view.
> 我需要男生的看法。

Jas

> Ok.
> 好。

小秘書

> Sue's boss wants her to join him on his biz trip.
> Sue 的老闆想要她和他一起出差。

Jas

> Where is he going?
> 他要去哪裡？

小秘書　　　　✐be into ~: 喜歡、對 ~ 有興趣

> Canada. I think he's pretty into her.
> 加拿大。我想他喜歡她。

Jas

> Maybe he just considers her a coworker or friend?
> 也許他只是把她當同事或朋友？

小秘書

> Friendship between men and women is impossible. Period.
> 男女之間沒有純友誼，以上。

Jas

Why not?
為什麼沒有？

小秘書

It's like cats and dogs. They can't be friends!
這就像貓和狗，牠們不可能會是朋友！

Jas

But they can be lovers?
但是牠們可以變戀人？

小秘書

You know what I mean!!
你明知道我的意思！！

✏whatever: 無論如何

Jas

Well, whatever.
Just don't forget to fill me in on the details!
無論如何，別忘了告訴我後續細節！

小秘書

Sure ;)
沒問題。

🔦 與分享消息有關的句子

That's what I'm curious about. 那點就是我好奇的。

Be cautious when posting personal information online. 在網路上放個人資料要小心。

Tell me how it happened in the first place. 告訴我一開始事情是怎麼發生的。

I really wanna remove my personal info from the website. 我真的想要從網路上刪除我的個人資料。

Teenagers tend to share too much info on FB. 青少年傾向在臉書上分享過多的資訊。

More to Talk!

Two-timing is not my thing.
我不是那種會劈腿的人。

小秘書

> Let's break up.
> 分手吧！

安琪兒

> What????
> 什麼？？？

小秘書 ✏ compatible: 互相適合

> We're not compatible.
> 我們不適合。

✏ Knock it off: 不要鬧了、住口 **安琪兒**

> Knock it off!
> 不要鬧了！

小秘書 ✏ mess up: 搞糟

> I'm rehearsing these things so I don't mess up.
> 我在練習以免搞糟。

安琪兒

> What's with you?
> 妳怎麼了？

小秘書

> You know I've been dating Hyun right?
> 妳知道我和 Hyun 在約會吧？

安琪兒

Of course. And?
當然，然後呢？

小秘書 🎵 on a date: 約會中

I saw him on a date with some other girl.
我看見他和其他女生約會。

🎵 no way: 不可能   安琪兒

No way!!! Such a player!
不可能！原來是花花公子啊！

小秘書

Maybe I should cheat to get back at him.
也許我應該劈回去。

🎵 Go for it: 上吧！開始吧！   安琪兒

Go for it!!!
上吧！！

小秘書   🎵 ~is not my thing: 我不是 ~ 的類型、我不是做 ~ 的料

No, two-timing is not my thing.
不行，我不是那種會劈腿的人。

More to Talk!

 與自制有關的句子

Cut it out. 別鬧了。
Stop it. 住手。
Cut the crap. 廢話少說。
Stay away. 離遠一點。
Move. 讓開。
Get off of me. 離我遠一點。

I made a faux pas.

我失態了。

Bean

> You're not going to stop laughing when I tell you this.
> 如果我告訴妳這件事，妳會笑得停不下來。

天鵝

> Tell me what?
> 告訴我什麼？

Bean ✏faux pas: 言行、舉止不得當 (源自法文)

> Let's just say I made a faux pas.
> 或者說是我失態了。

天鵝

> Spill.
> 說吧！

Bean ✏chat up: 搭訕、調情

> So, my nightmare boss...
> I wanted to see if I could chat him up a little.
> 就是說我那個可怕的老闆…我想試試看是否我能和他聊個幾句。

✏jerk: 討厭鬼 (較輕微的罵人用詞) 天鵝

> WHAT?! WHY?! He's such a jerk!
> 什麼？為什麼？他完全討人厭啊！

Bean ✏figure: 認為、推測

> Yeah but he's a hot jerk. And I figured maybe he would start being nicer.
> 沒錯，但他是一個性感的討厭鬼，我想也許他會開始變好。

天鵝

> I knew you had a crush on him. Well???
> 我知道妳曾被他煞到，然後？

Bean

✎flirt with ~: 打情罵俏、送秋波

> I was flirting with him when we were closing up the café. I must have been out of my mind. And then he had a piece of fuzz on his shirt.
> 在我們關店時，我和他打情罵俏，我一定是瘋了，他的襯衫有一點起毛球。

✎pick something off: 摘掉   天鵝

> So... you picked it off? lol
> 所以…妳摘掉了？呵呵

Bean

> And I heard a noise. When I turned around there was a woman at the door. His WIFE!
> 然後我聽到一個聲音，當我往後看，有個女人在門邊，他的太太！！

✎You can't make things like this up!: 妳不可能編出這種事！不會是編的吧？   天鵝

> lolllllllllllllll You can't make things like this up!
> 呵呵呵呵呵，不會是編的吧？

與社會生活&禮貌有關的句子

Smoking in front of your boss is bad manners. 在你的老闆面前抽菸是沒有禮貌的事。

It's inappropriate to wear miniskirts to work. 在公司不適合穿迷你裙。

Being late is rude but being too early is also a bad idea. 遲到很沒禮貌，但早到也不好。

Bringing a gift for the host or hostess is proper etiquette. 帶禮物去拜訪人家是種禮貌。

If you can't make it then you should at least call. 如果你不能去，至少你應該打個電話。

He's still hung up on his ex. 他仍然想著前女友。

 Tae

What's with King_Michael? He seems really bummed lately.
King_Michael 怎麼了？他最近似乎很鬱悶。

🎵hung up on ~: 掛念 ~　　　　　　　　　　　　電玩宅

He's still hung up on his ex. They broke up a few weeks ago and he can't seem to move on.
他仍然想著前女友，他們幾星期前分手了，他似乎不能忘懷。

 Tae　🎵dang: damn 的委婉表現，該死的、可惡

Dang. What happened?
該死的，發生了什麼事？

🎵dump: 傾倒 / take it: 接受　　　　　　　　　電玩宅

She dumped him by text. He didn't take it very well.
她用文字甩了他。他很難接受。

 Tae　　　　　　　🎵sux: sucks 的簡寫

That sux. There's plenty of fish in the sea though.
太爛了，反正還有很多合適的人選。

電玩宅

I tried telling him that. He didn't appreciate it.
我試著那樣跟他說，但他不領情。

Tae
combo: combination 的縮寫

Hmm. Perhaps we should take him out this Sat. We can do the 3 spot combo.
嗯，也許我們星期六應該帶他出去，我們可以玩 3 攤。

電玩宅

3 spot combo?
3 攤？

Tae

bar, club, singing room.
酒吧、夜店、KTV。

電玩宅

Hahaha. I'm down.
哈哈哈，我輸了。

Tae

Alright I'll send him a text n see what he thinks.
好，我會傳訊息看他要不要。

電玩宅

Cool.
好的。

 與玩樂有關的句子

I'll get the next round if you go talk to that girl.
如果你去搭訕那個女生，下一攤我就請客。

I'm tired of this place. Let's move to another spot.
我厭倦了這個地方，換其他地方吧！

That place is full of hotties.
那個地方有很多正妹。

ChitChat **026**   p 72

Love is one thing and marriage is another.

sign up with ~ 加入
matchmaking agency 婚姻介紹所
decent 不錯的
go for 喜歡、選擇
practical 實際的
go out with ~ 和 ~ 約會
Love is one thing and marriage is another. 愛情和婚姻是兩回事。
calculating 善於算計的
super busy with ~ 因 ~ 超級忙碌
arrange 安排
focus on ~ 集中於 ~
win-win situation 雙贏局面
blind date 相親
ask someone out 要求和某人約會
love marriage 戀愛結婚
arranged marriage 相親結婚
get back together 復合

ChitChat **027**   p 74

It's not like I have a ring on my finger.

on a date 約會中
It's not like I have a ring on my finger.
還不到套上戒指的程度。
out of the loop 感到像局外人
grab a coffee 喝杯咖啡

girl talk 女孩之間的聊天
Gotta go! 必須去！
exclusive 交往中的
settle down 穩定
committed relationship 有承諾的關係

ChitChat **028**   p 76

She won't give me the time of day.

She won't give me the time of day.
她從來不給我機會。
have a crush 被 ~ 煞到
crush 著迷
little brother 弟弟
Don't patronize. 少來這套
have feelings for~ 對 ~ 有感覺
have a thing for~ 喜歡 ~
more than just friends 不只是朋友

ChitChat **029**   p 78

What's with you lately?

bro brother 朋友
What's with you lately? 你最近怎麼了？
return one's calls 回電
answer one's texts 回訊息
respond to one's messages 回訊息
Are you ignoring me? 你不理我嗎？
hang up 掛電話
turn off one's phone 關機

ChitChat 030

p 80

Pull yourself together.

make a mistake 犯錯

make the first move 首先開始

out of one's mind 精神不正常

breathe 呼吸

Pull yourself together. 冷靜下來。

regret 後悔

Stop regretting your decision. 不要後悔妳的決定。

feel sorry for 對 ~ 感到遺憾

one last time 最後一次

careless 輕率的

wasted time 浪費時間

ChitChat 031

p 82

It was a total disaster!

set someone up 安排相親

How'd it go? 後來如何了？

It was a total disaster. 完全是個災難！

talk one's ear off saying that ~ 說 ~ 說到我耳朵長繭

way too high 太高了

have a conversation with 和 ~ 對話

reject 拒絕

hottie 正妹

shallow 膚淺的

stuck 困住的

The worst part is over. 最糟的部份已經結束了。

one way or another 某種方式

ChitChat 032

p 84

Epic fail

give up 放棄

impress 使印象深刻

follow one's advice 按照 ~ 的建議

make a fool of oneself 讓某人出醜

fancy-schmancy 非常華麗誇張的

bitter 苦的

barely 幾乎不 ~

knock 打翻

shatter 破碎

scream 尖叫

wreck 毀壞

epic fail 史上最糟糕

idiot 白癡、笨蛋

mortified 羞恥的

show one's face 露面

What a clown! 太愚蠢了！

humiliating 羞恥的

ChitChat 033

p 86

It's just not working.

lately 最近

It's just not working. 行不通的。

break up with someone by text message 用簡訊和 ~ 分手

Whatever. 隨你便。

Can we start over? 我們不能重新開始嗎？

give someone another chance 再給我一次機會

without a fight 不爭取

p 88

ChitChat 034

Friendship between men and women is impossible. Period.

point of view 觀點、立場

biz trip 出差

be into ~ 喜歡、對 ~ 有興趣

Friendship between men and women is impossible. Period. 男女之間沒有純友誼，以上。

It's like cats and dogs. 就像貓和狗的關係。

fill someone in on~ 告訴 ~ 有關 ~

curious 好奇的

in the first place 一開始

ChitChat 035

p 90

Two-timing is not my thing.

compatible 互相適合

knock it off 不要鬧了

Such a player! 原來是花花公子！

cheat 劈腿、欺騙

get back at ~ 報復 ~

Go for it! 上吧！

two-timing 劈腿

Two-timing is not my thing. 我不是那種會劈腿的人。

ChitChat 036

p 92

I made a faux pas.

I made a faux pas. 我失態了。

nightmare 惡夢

chat up 搭訕

jerk 討厭鬼

flirt 打情罵俏、送秋波

fuzz 毛球

make up 編造

inappropriate 不適合的

ChitChat 037

p 94

He's still hung up on his ex.

bummed 鬱鬱寡歡的

ex 前男 / 女友

He's still hung up on his ex. 他仍然想著前女友。

move on 忘懷

dump 傾倒、丟棄

dump by text 用文字分手

There's plenty of fish in the sea. 還有其他合適的人或機會。

take someone out 帶 ~ 出去

spot 場所

combo combination 的縮寫

go clubbing 去夜店

ritzy 高級的

get the next round 下一攤請客

I'll get the next round. 下一攤我請客。

CHAT
04
Health & Food
健康與食物

Speak for yourself.

那是你自己的看法。

 Jas

> Can't sleep.
> 睡不著。

Kell2013

> Too much coffee?
> 喝太多咖啡了？

 Jas

🎵 sort of: 大概、就那樣、有點

> Sort of.
> 有點。

🎵 coffee addict: 咖啡上癮者   Kell2013

> No offense, but you're a coffee addict.
> 無意冒犯，但你是咖啡上癮者啊。

 Jas

> Speak for yourself.
> 那是你自己的看法。

🎵 w/o: without 的簡稱   Kell2013

> He he. But I just can't wake myself up w/o a morning coffee.
> 嘿嘿，不過我沒有早晨咖啡就醒不來。

Jas

*Same here: 我也是

Same here.
我也是。

*w: with 的簡稱

Kell2013

Speaking of which, r u ready for the presentation?
說到這個，你的簡報準備好了嗎？

Jas

*born ready: 一出生就準備好了、完全準備好了

Of course. I was born ready.
當然，我完全準備好了。

Kell2013

Good.
太好了。

More to Talk!

 有 oneself 的句子

Don't be so hard on yourself. 不要太自責了。

Give yourself a little credit. 給自己一點自信。

He started to talk to himself. 他開始自言自語。

Take a good look at yourself in the mirror. 你看看鏡子裡的自己。

He prides himself on his good looks. 他對自己的外貌很自豪。

He lives off Instant noodles and soda. 他靠泡麵和汽水維生。

King_Michael

I'm too tired to meet tonight.
我今天太累，不能見面。

✐Spent: I spent 的縮寫

Tae

Me too. Spent all my energy at the gym.
我也是，我在健身房把力氣用完了。

電玩宅

✐~suck: 差勁、糟透

What?! You guys suck.
什麼？你們這些遜咖。

King_Michael

Sorry. It's just part of getting old.
抱歉，這是年紀變大的表現。

Tae

Ha! Yeah, I don't have energy like I used to.
哈！沒錯，我不像以前那樣有體力了。

電玩宅

WOW You two sound like senior citizens...
Forget you guys! I'm gonna be up all night.
哇，你們兩個聽起來像老人…別再說了你們！我晚上要去熬夜了。

King_Michael

Ohhh What's your secret?
喔～你的秘訣是什麼？

🖉live off: 靠～維生

Tae

He lives off Instant noodles and soda.
他靠泡麵和汽水維生。

電玩宅

Hahaha yeah. I call it the PC Room Diet.
哈哈哈，嗯，我稱為網咖減肥法。

King_Michael　🖉LMAO: Laughing My Ass Off (ass 這個詞較低俗，只用於熟悉的朋友) 笑死

LMAO
笑死。

電玩宅

You should try it. I'm always energized. ;)
你應該試看看，我總是體力充沛～

Tae

lol
呵呵

More to Talk!

與恢復體力有關的句子

I stopped drinking energy drinks because they were giving me headaches. 我不再喝能量飲料了，因為它讓我頭痛。

Coffee doesn't agree with me. 咖啡不適合我。

The doctor gave me a vitamin shot to help with the fatigue. 醫生給我打了維他命點滴以幫助恢復疲勞。

Too much caffeine will have you up all night. 太多的咖啡因會使你整晚睡不著。

CHAT 04 **103**

What exactly is that?

那個究竟是什麼？

Kell2013

> I invited my friends from the States to my place for dinner and I have no idea what to serve.
> 我邀請從美國來的朋友到我家吃晚餐，但我不知道要招待什麼。

🔖 Give'em: Give them 的縮寫　　　　　　　　　　　　　**Jas**

> Give'em Bulgogi! It's always a hit w/ our foreign clients.
> 給他們吃韓式烤肉！這是我們公司外國客戶最喜歡的。

Kell2013

🔖 vegan: 純素主義者

> Can't. They're vegan. No meat.
> 不行，他們吃全素，不吃肉。

🔖 vegetarian: 素食主義者　　　　　　　　　　　　　　**Jas**

> Vegan? What exactly is that? Is it like being a vegetarian?
> 全素？那個究竟是什麼？類似素食主義者？

Kell2013

> Like a vegetarian but stricter. No eggs, no cheese. No animal products of any sort.
> 比素食主義者更嚴格，不吃雞蛋、起司、以及任何產自動物的產品。

🔖 kudos: 讚美　　　　　　　　　　　　　　　　　　　**Jas**

> Wow. Well kudos to them for their healthy lifestyle. Unfortunately it sounds like your menu options are pretty limited.
> 哇，稱嘆他們的健康生活方式，但不幸地這聽起來妳的菜單非常受到限制。

Kell2013

soup broth: 高湯

Yeah. And everything I know how to make has seafood or eggs. :(They can't even eat soup broth made with anchovies.
嗯，而且我會做的料理都有海鮮或雞蛋 :(他們甚至不能喝用小鯷魚熬的高湯。

Jas

Guess you'll have to go with bibimbap. Minus the egg, of course.
我想妳得做拌飯了，當然要去掉雞蛋。

Kell2013

And dessert?
那麼甜點呢？

Jas

Fresh fruit and tea? I bet they've never tried chamoe melon before.
新鮮水果和茶？我打賭他們從來沒吃過甜香瓜。

Kell2013

Good idea. I knew you'd be the person to ask.
好主意，我就知道問對人了。

 與健康食品有關的句子

He is striving to eat more unprocessed foods for his health. 他為了健康，努力攝取更多未經加工過的食物。

We switched to soy milk when we heard about growth hormones in regular milk. 聽到一般牛奶裡含有生長賀爾蒙後，我們改喝豆漿。

Choose the juice with the least amount of additives for your children. 為了你的孩子，選擇添加物最少的果汁。

Many housewives purchase more expensive organic produce in hopes of preventing cancer. 許多家庭主婦購買較昂貴的有機產品，期望能預防癌症。

I'm not sure what she's into.

我不確定她喜歡什麼。

Tae

> I need your help.
> 我需要你的幫忙。

電玩宅

> With?
> 哪種？

Tae

> I've got a date and I don't know where to take her.
> I'm not sure what she's into.
> 我有個約會，但我不知道要帶她去哪裡，我不確定她喜歡什麼。

♫I'm not good with ~: 我不擅長 ~   電玩宅

> U know I'm not very good with the ladies.
> 你知道我不擅長女生這方面。

Tae

> You gotta have some idea...
> 你會有些主意的…

Tae

> Well I know what movie she wants to see.
> It's dinner I don't know what to do about.
> 我知道她想要看什麼電影，就是晚餐我不知道要怎麼辦。

電玩宅

> How about Italian? Girls love pasta. Or so I hear...
> 義大利料理如何？女生都喜歡義大利麵，至少我是這樣聽說…

Tae

Hmm...
嗯…

🎵 ~or something: 類似那樣的

Otherwise something trendy. Like Indian or something.
不然就最近流行的，類似印度料理那樣的。

電玩宅

Tae

You think she'd go for a Brazilian steakhouse? Unlimited meat.
你覺得她會喜歡巴西式牛排嗎？肉吃到飽。

🎵 She's not into it: 她不會喜歡的。

If she's not into it you can always date me ;)
如果她不喜歡的話，你可以和我約會 ;)

電玩宅

Tae

lol Ur not my type.
呵呵，你不是我的菜。

 與異國料理有關的句子

More to Talk!

Most places serve frozen stuff but their sushi is all fresh. 大部份的餐廳都是冷凍食材，但他們的壽司全都是新鮮的。

How about something exotic like Thai or Vietnamese? 像泰國或越南那樣的異國料理如何？

The curry at the Indian place near my office is amazing! 公司附近的印度餐廳的咖哩很令人驚豔！

There are Chinese restaurants everywhere but it's hard to find an authentic one. 雖然到處都是中國餐廳，但要找到道地的很難。

Instead of a big meal let's go for something light like wine and tapas.
不要吃大餐，去吃像酒和小菜那樣的輕食吧！

What should I eat to up my stamina?
我該吃什麼來增強體力？

小秘書

Whew! It's steamy hot!!!
呼～真是太悶熱了！！

安琪兒

Tell me about it.
可不是嗎？

小秘書

What can I eat to up my stamina?
我該吃什麼來增強體力？

✎ dunno: don't know 的網路用語　安琪兒

I dunno. Grilled eel?
我不知道，烤鰻魚？

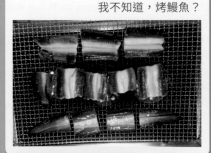

小秘書 🎵have a strong stomach: 有個強健的胃

Ewww! You sure have a strong stomach!
喂！妳真的有個強健的胃。

🎵~will do: ~ 就可以、~ 就夠了　安琪兒

Maybe samgyetang will do.
也許蔘雞湯可以。

小秘書　🎵(Are you) up for ~: 對 ~ 有興趣嗎？

Up for samgyetang, then?
那麼要去吃蔘雞湯嗎？

安琪兒

Sure. The usual spot?
好啊，老地方？

 與炎熱有關的句子

Hitting the movies is a good way to survive sizzling summer days. 在炎熱的夏天要生存，看電影是好方法。

I can't stand this hot, humid weather! 我不能忍受這個又濕又熱的天氣！

I'd rather it be freezing than scorching. I can always layer on more clothes. 我寧願凍死也不要熱死，我可以多包幾層衣服就好。

I'm all sweaty. How do I stop my makeup from melting? 我滿身大汗，我要怎樣才能不讓妝糊掉呢？

Look. I'm sweating like a pig. 看，我滿身大汗。

I occasionally splurge on weekends. 我週末偶爾會暴食。

Kell2013

> You're looking thinner these days.
> 妳最近看起來變瘦了。

安琪兒

> Am I?
> 我嗎？

Kell2013

> What's the big secret?
> 秘訣是什麼？

安琪兒

> The Half Food Diet.
> 吃一半。

Kell2013

> Isn't that tough?
> 不辛苦嗎？

安琪兒

> You know it.
> 妳知道的。

Kell2013

🖉 OMG: Oh, my god 的縮寫，我的天啊！

> OMG, how can U not be tempted?
> 我的天啊！妳怎能不被誘惑？

🖉 splurge: 暴食   安琪兒

> I occasionally splurge on weekends. HaHa.
> 我週末偶爾會暴食。哈哈。

Kell2013

> LOL. Honestly, I would be tempted.
> 呵呵，說真的，如果是我就會忍不住。

安琪兒

What's that saying again....
那個是怎麼說的…

Kell2013

What?
什麼？

🎵Hara hachi bu: 日本諺語，意指「只吃八分飽」。　安琪兒

"Hara hachi bu?"
"Hara hachi bu?" 嗎？

Kell2013　　　🎵yep: yes 的口語。

Yep. "Eat until you feel 80% full."
嗯，「只吃八分飽」。

安琪兒

Eating less is good for you anyway.
反正少吃一點對妳是好的。

與減肥有關的句子

She's lost a ton of weight on the Lemon Detox Diet. 她用檸檬排毒減肥餐瘦了很多。

The vocal trainee is on a protein only diet before his debut. 這個歌手練習生在出道之前正進行蛋白質減肥法。

An unbalanced diet leads to malnutrition. 不均衡的減肥法會導致營養失調。

The actor got hooked on diet pills. 那個演員迷上減肥藥了。

She's trying to get her figure back after childbirth. 她在產後嘗試恢復體態。

Diets are rarely successful in the long run because of the yo-yo effect.
因為溜溜球效應，所以長期來說減肥很難成功。

More to Talk!

The meat was dry and the veggies were all mushy. 肉很乾,蔬菜也太軟爛了。

Jas

The new Italian restaurant sucks!
新的義大利餐廳很糟!

小秘書

The one on the Zhongyang Road?
在中央路那家嗎?

Jas

Yes. I ordered the lunch special.
對,我點了午餐特餐。

小秘書

And?
然後?

Jas

🖊veggies: vegetables 的簡稱

The meat was dry and the veggies were all mushy.
肉很乾,蔬菜也太軟爛了。

小秘書

Sounds horrible.
聽起來很糟。

Jas

And the servers are rude, too.
而且服務也很不好。

♪déjà vu: 似曾相識的感覺　小秘書

Déjà vu.
有似曾相識的感覺。

Jas

What?
什麼？

小秘書

That sounds just like the old restaurant there.
聽起來跟那裡原本的餐廳一樣。

Jas　　　　　　　　　♪last: 持續的

Hmmm…. That place didn't last that long.
嗯…那個餐廳沒有開很久。

小秘書

Let's see if the new place gets any better.
看看新餐廳是否會變好。

More to Talk!

與美食有關的句子

I have a craving for some scrumptious apple pie. 我很想吃超好吃的蘋果派。

The seafood there was to die for. 那裡的海鮮超級好吃。

Thanks for the yummy cookies. 謝謝給我好吃的餅乾。

I'm drooling as I think of their naengmyeon. 冷麵光用想的就流口水了。

Let me show you how to make mouth-watering bibimbap. 讓我告訴你如何做出令人垂涎三尺的拌飯。

Do they have any lo-cal options?
他們有低卡路里食物嗎？

天鵝

Buffet tonight?
今晚自助餐如何？

🎵Sry: sorry 的簡稱　　安琪兒

Can't. Sry.
不能去，抱歉。

天鵝

Tomorrow?
明天呢？

安琪兒

I'm not sure...
我不確定…

天鵝

You've been talking about going to this place for like two weeks!
兩個星期來妳一直在說要去這家餐廳！

安琪兒

That was before I tried on my clothes from last summer...
那是在我試穿去年夏天的衣服之前說的…

天鵝

✏️Gotcha.: 我懂了

Gotcha. lol Italian then? That place by my house finally opened.

懂了，呵呵。那麼義大利料理？我家附近的那家餐廳終於開幕了。

✏️Depends = It depends. / lo-cal = low calories

安琪兒

Depends. Do they have any lo-cal options?

不一定會去，他們有低卡路里食物嗎？

天鵝

They probably have something. I'll call and find out.

他們應該會有吧。我打電話問問看。

安琪兒

Thanks! :D

謝謝 ^^

 與營養資訊有關的句子

With this diet plan you have to count calories. 這個減肥計畫需要計算卡路里。

Eat foods low in saturated fat and cut down on sugar. 吃飽和脂肪低的食物和減少糖份攝取。

They use artificial sweetener instead of sugar to save calories. 他們使用代糖取代糖以降低卡路里。

She lost 2 kilos by eating whole grains such as brown rice instead of white rice. 她吃全穀類，例如糙米取代白米，就瘦了 2 公斤。

Take a multivitamin to ensure you're getting the proper amount of vitamins and minerals. 吃綜合維他命以確保你能獲得適量的維他命和礦物質。

More to Talk!

My stomach is growling.

我的胃在咕嚕咕嚕叫。

 小秘書

> I'm so hungry!!!
> 我好餓！！

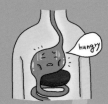

🔊 hr: hour 的簡稱　　　Kell2013

> What??? U ate less than an hr ago.
> 什麼？妳不到一小時前才吃了東西。

 小秘書　🔊 growling: 低聲咆哮

> My stomach is growling.
> 我的胃在咕嚕咕嚕叫。

Kell2013

> Eat.
> 吃啊。

 小秘書

> There's nothing to eat.
> 沒有東西可以吃。

Kell2013

> Come to think of it, didn't you start a diet?
> 這樣一想，妳不是在減肥嗎？

 小秘書　🔊 That' why ~.: 所以

> That's why I emptied my fridge.
> 所以我清空了冰箱。

I'm getting hungry.
我也變餓了。

小秘書　♪order in: 叫外送

Order in pizza.
來叫披薩。

Kell2013

Yeah, sounds good.
好，聽起來不錯。

小秘書

Ugh, I think I'm regaining my appetite!
啊～～ 我又有胃口了！

♪lost an appetite: 失去胃口　Kell2013

Like you've ever lost it.
妳哪時沒胃口了。

小秘書　♪Can I come over (to your place)?: 可以去你家嗎？

...can I come over? ....
我可以過去嗎？

More to Talk!

 與飢餓口渴有關的句子

I'm starving to death. 我快餓死了。

He was extremely thirsty after working out. 他運動後非常口渴。

He's starved for love. 他渴望愛情。

Can sports drinks quench your thirst better than water? 運動飲料比水更能解渴嗎？

Cigarettes may help decrease your appetite. 香菸可能會降低你的食慾。

Hunger is the best appetizer. 飢餓是最好的開胃菜。

What are you in the mood for?

妳想吃什麼？

小秘書

So, when and where?
那麼何時何地呢？

Kell2013

7ish?
7 點？

小秘書

K. Then where?
OK，那麼在哪裡？

Kell2013

What are you in the mood for?
妳想吃什麼？

小秘書　✎ light: 輕的、無負擔的

Anything light. U?
輕食都可以。妳呢？

✎ Me 2.: Me too. 的網路用語。　Kell2013

Me 2. I'm avoiding carbs these days.
我也是，我最近少吃碳水化合物。

小秘書

Salad?
沙拉？

✎ You read my mind: 你最懂我、同意、好的　Kell2013

You read my mind.
妳懂我。

小秘書 🖉vegetarian: 素食主義者的

Know any good vegetarian restaurants?
知道有什麼不錯的素食餐廳嗎？

Kell2013

I know one in Yilan.
我知道宜蘭有一家。

小秘書 🖉caught in traffic: 塞車

Too far. Plus I don't wanna get caught in traffic.
太遠了，而且我不想塞車。

Kell2013

Good point.
說得不錯。

 與塞車有關的句子

There's nothing worse than being stuck in traffic. 沒有比塞車更糟的事情了。

Let's hit the road now and beat the rush hour traffic. 現在就上路避免塞車。

I sat in traffic for more than 5 hours. 我困在車陣裡超過 5 小時了。

He prefers public transportation to avoid Monday morning rush hour.
他較喜歡搭大眾交通以避開星期一的尖峰時間。

It was bumper-to-bumper all the way to work. 到公司的路總是車多。

You're hitting the gym pretty hard. 你很勤跑健身房。

King_Michael 🔗Where u at?: Where are you at? 的縮寫 (不合文法，但可用於熟人)

Where u at?
你在哪？

Tae

Why? Lol
怎麼了？呵呵。

King_Michael

Thought you were coming out for drinks?
以為你會來喝一杯？

🔗stop off: 中途停留 / tho: though 的簡稱 Tae

At the gym now. I might stop off after tho.
現在在健身房。等一下可能會過去一下。

King_Michael 🔗hit the gym: 去健身房

You're hitting the gym pretty hard these days.
你最近很勤跑健身房。

🔗bod: body 的簡稱，身體 / Esp: especially 的簡稱，特別地 Tae

Gotta work on my beach body. Lol Esp before my Jeju trip.
要去鍛鍊海灘男孩的身體了，呵呵，特別是在去濟洲島旅行之前。

King_Michael

Lol Yeah, I hear you. Been meaning to hit the gym myself.
呵呵，我知道了，我也在想要不要去健身房。

Tae

🖊come with: come with me 的縮寫

You should come with.
你應該一起來。

King_Michael 🖊cardio: cardiovascular 的簡稱、心血管的

You doing weight training or cardio?
你做重量訓練還是有氧運動？

Tae

🖊Two birds with one stone.: 一石二鳥

Both. Circuit training. Two birds with one stone.
都做，循環訓練，一石二鳥。

King_Michael

Nice.
不錯呢。

More to Talk!

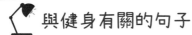 **與健身有關的句子**

I do 100 crunches every night to tone my abs. 我每天晚上做 100 次仰臥起坐以強化腹部。

Circuit training is the best way to burn fat and build muscle. 循環訓練是燃燒脂肪和鍛鍊肌肉的最好方法。

He has been doing pushups to build up his upper arms, shoulders, and chest. 他做伏地挺身以鍛鍊他的上臂、肩膀和胸部。

I heard doing squats is a great way to work on your lower body. 我聽說深蹲是鍛鍊下半身的好方法。

Strength and endurance are important but a lot of people forget to work on flexibility as well. 雖然力量和耐力很重要，但很多人都忘了練習柔軟度。

My head is killing me.

我的頭痛死了。

Bean

Why aren't you answering your phone?
妳怎麼沒接電話？

天鵝

My head is killing me.
我的頭痛死了。

Bean

What's wrong? You sick?
怎麼了？妳生病了？

天鵝

No. I'm okay.
沒有，沒事。

Bean

I hear the flu is going around.
Need me to bring you some porridge or something?
我聽說流感正在流行，需要我帶點粥之類的給妳嗎？

天鵝

It's not the flu. I just had a few too many last night.
不是流感，我只是昨晚喝多了。

Bean

I thought you went home right after work?
我以為妳下班後就馬上回家了。

天鵝

A friend called me out last minute.
有個朋友最後打電話來了。

Bean

Lol I'll be over in a few with some aspirin and Instant noodles.
呵呵，我等一下會帶阿斯匹靈和泡麵過去。

天鵝

Ur the best.
妳最棒了。

Bean

What would you do without me? :P
沒有我妳要怎麼辦？（吐舌頭）

與小病有關的句子

More to Talk!

Just take some OTC drugs and you'll be better in no time. 吃點藥局的藥，妳會馬上好的。

Be careful. I hear there's a stomach virus going around. 小心，我聽說正在流行腸胃炎。

I've come down with a cold and can't go to work. 我感冒不能去上班。

It's just a little bug. I'll be fine. 我只是小感冒，沒事的。

The doctor gave me a prescription for my sinus cold. 醫生為我的鼻炎開了處方箋。

I'm quitting alcohol cold turkey!

我要戒酒！

Jas

I'm dying.
我快死了。

Kell2013

Why?
為什麼？

Jas

I drank too much last night.
我昨晚喝太多了。

Kell2013

Again? Another company dinner?
又一次？公司又聚餐了？

Jas

soju bombs: 炸彈酒

Yes. We did soju bombs until late.
對，我們喝炸彈酒喝到很晚。

Kell2013

You guys seem to get together every Friday night.
你們似乎每個星期五晚上都聚餐。

Jas

I don't feel comfortable at office dinners,
but it's hard to say no.
雖然我對公司聚餐感到不自在，但很難說不。

Kell2013

Totally agree with you.
我完全同意。

Jas 🗝sleep the hangover off: 用睡眠來解宿醉

I just wanna sleep this hangover off.
我只想要用睡眠來解宿醉。

Kell2013

Go for it. You need to prepare for the next one. :P
去吧！你需要準備下一次。（吐舌頭）

Jas 🗝quit cold turkey: 戒斷

No! I'm quitting alcohol cold turkey!
不！我要戒酒！

Kell2013

Easier said than done.
說的比做容易。

 與喝酒有關的句子

Let's have a toast! 乾杯！

I can't hold my liquor at all. 我完全不會喝酒。

Do you know about the dog hair remedy? 你知道解宿醉的方法嗎？

What's the best way to avoid a hangover? 避免宿醉最好的方法是什麼？

Drunk drivers often cause high speed collisions. 喝酒開車經常超速造成車禍。

I tripped texting and walking.

我走路打字時絆倒了。

小秘書

> Bad news.
> 壞消息。

Jas

> What?
> 什麼？

小秘書

> I sprained my left ankle.
> 我扭傷了左踝。

Jas

> How?
> 怎麼弄的？

小秘書

🖉trip: 絆倒

> I tripped while texting and walking.
> 我走路打字時絆倒了。

Jas

> HA! You were asking for it!
> 嘿！妳是自找的！

小秘書

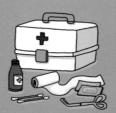

> I'm in a half cast.
> 我打了一半石膏。

Jas

Is it very swollen?
腫得很大嗎?

小秘書 ✏n: and 的簡稱 / black and blue: 瘀腫的

Swollen n black and blue.
又腫又黑青。

Jas

So, no more high heels?
所以不能再穿高跟鞋了?

小秘書

They're a no-no for now. At least my phone survived.
現在不行了,至少我的手機還是好的。

Jas

LOL Thank God!!!
呵呵,謝天謝地!!

More to Talk!

 與骨折、脫臼有關的句子

I broke my leg. 我腳斷了。

I pulled a muscle in my leg. 我韌帶拉傷了。

He dislocated his shoulder while snowboarding. 他滑雪時把肩膀弄脫臼了。

She twisted her ankle running. 她跑步時扭傷腳踝了。

I threw my back out. 我閃到腰了。

My head feels foggy.

我覺得意識模糊。

Kell2013

✏ panic attack: 恐慌症

How do you know if ur having a panic attack?
妳怎麼知道妳有恐慌症呢？

安琪兒

Umm..u have lots of stress n start freaking out? lol
嗯…妳會感到壓力很大，開始崩潰？呵呵

Kell2013

My head feels foggy and I can't stop sweating.
I feel a little nauseous too.
我覺得意識模糊，不停流汗，也感到有點噁心。

安琪兒

What??! OMG
什麼？我的天啊！

Kell2013

I tried calling someone but my words
weren't coming out right.
我嘗試打電話給人，但說不出話來。

✏ r u = are you   安琪兒

Where r u?
妳在哪裡？

Kell2013

Home
家。

安琪兒

I'll be right there. I'll take you to the ER.
我馬上到，我帶妳去急診。

Kell2013

K
知道了。

安琪兒

Sit down and just try to breathe deep.
坐下，試著深呼吸。

Kell2013

K
嗯。

安琪兒

Just hang on. I'm coming.
忍一下，我馬上到。

與症狀有關的句子

If you're feeling dizzy, sit down. 如果你覺得頭暈，就坐下。

I am having trouble concentrating and I get upset very easily.
我無法集中精神，容易感到沮喪。

He seems really forgetful these days. 他最近似乎很健忘。

I'm really tired and sluggish lately so I made a doctor's appointment.
我最近很疲倦、無精打采，所以我預約了醫生。

If it gets worse you should see a doctor immediately. 如果變得嚴重，你應
該立刻去看醫生。

Worry can make you sick.

憂慮會讓你生病。

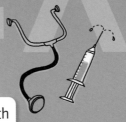

小秘書

I heard about what happened with Kell2013. Is everything okay?
我聽說 Kell2013 發生的事了。她還好嗎？

安琪兒

Yeah. She's okay. We're at the hospital now.
嗯，她還好，我們現在在醫院。

小秘書

So what did they say is the problem?
所以問題是什麼？

安琪兒

The doctor said it's just stress.
醫生說她只是壓力大。

小秘書

That's going to be hard for her, being a workaholic and all.
這對她來說很困難，她是工作狂。

安琪兒

They gave her a prescription and told her to take a few days off work.
他們給她處方箋，告訴她要休息幾天。

小秘書

How'd she take that?
她怎麼會接受？

安琪兒

Well, she started talking about who would take care of her projects.
她開始談論誰來負責她的案子。

小秘書

OMG
喔喔！

安琪兒

🖊be worried about: 擔心～

She is just really worried about work.
她真的很擔心工作。

小秘書

Jeez! This is really serious!
我的天！這很嚴重！

安琪兒

Yeah. :' (Her mom is going to come n take care of her for a few days.
對，她媽媽會來照顧她幾天。

小秘書

That's a relief. So what they say is true... worry can make you sick.
真是鬆了一口氣，所以那句話是對的…憂慮會讓妳生病。

安琪兒

She'll be better after a few days. No better cure than rest and Mom's home cooking.
她幾天就會好的。沒有什麼比休息和媽媽的飯菜更好的了。

小秘書

So true.
沒錯。

與消除壓力有關的句子

Why don't you go away for the weekend to relieve some stress?
你週末要不要出去順便減輕壓力？

I like to work off my stress by going for a run. 我喜歡用跑步來消除壓力。

Whenever I get really stressed out I like to go hiking or do some other outdoor activity. 每當我感到壓力時，我喜歡去登山或做一些戶外活動。

The best way to beat stress is to spend time with friends. 消除壓力最好的方法是和朋友在一起。

I avoid stressful situations whenever possible. 我避免可能會帶來壓力的情況。

More to Talk!

I'll keep my fingers crossed.

我會為你祈禱。

 Tae   🖊big day: 大日子

> **Today's the big day.**
> 今天是我的大日子。

Jas

> **Oh?**
> 嗯。

Tae

> **I'm taking King_Michael to the dentist.**
> 我要帶 King_Michael 去看牙科。

Jas

> **So what?**
> 又怎麼樣？

Tae   🖊apparently: 明顯地

> **He hasn't gone in 10 years. Apparently he's deathly afraid.**
> 他 10 年沒去了，很明顯他害怕。

🖊srsly: (seriously) 真的嗎？   Jas

> **Hahahaha Srsly?**
> 哈哈哈，真的嗎？

 Tae   🖊I kid you not.: 不是開玩笑

> **I kid you not.**
> 我不是開玩笑。

Jas

> **What's the big deal?**
> 大日子是什麼？

Tae

fill a cavity: 補蛀牙

Some childhood fear... Had a dentist fill a cavity when he was young and it went all wrong.
因為一些童年的恐懼⋯他小時候給牙醫補過牙，完全是一團糟。

Jas

Poor little guy :P Everything will be fine. lol
可憐的小傢伙（吐舌）。一切都會順利的。

Tae

I booked with the gentlest dentist in town. Just hope he actually shows and doesn't leave me hanging. Or worse...run out of the place screaming!
我預約了鎮上最溫柔的牙醫，只希望他會來，別把我一個人晾著，或是更糟⋯尖叫著跑出去！

Jas

lol I'll keep my fingers crossed.
呵呵，我會為你禱告。

 與牙齒保健有關的句子

My dentist always scolds me for not flossing. 我的牙醫總是責罵我不用牙線。

Brush your teeth after every meal and use a good mouthwash. 每餐飯後要刷牙和使用好的漱口水。

I'm thinking about getting my teeth professionally whitened. 我正在考慮接受專業的牙齒美白。

She had braces up until she was 17 and still has to wear a retainer at night. 她戴牙套戴到 17 歲，現在每天晚上也必須戴著。

They had to pull all of his wisdom teeth at once. 他們必須一次拔掉他的智齒。

You'll be back to normal in no time.
你會馬上好轉的。

Jas

I may have to postpone my trip to Hong Kong.
我可能必須把香港旅行延期。

Tae

Really? But you've been looking forward to it!
真的？但你一直很期待啊！

Jas

🔖 take its toll: 造成損失

Yeah but I think all this work is starting to take its toll.
嗯，但我想最近的工作已經開始造成影響了。

🔖 lemme= let me

Tae

Lemme guess... Your neck again?
讓我猜猜看…你的脖子又發作了？

Jas

You guessed it. I've tried everything but no luck.
你猜對了。我什麼都嘗試了，但沒用。

🔖 acupuncture: 針炙

Tae

What about acupuncture?
針灸如何？

Jas

Hmm... That's a thought! Know any Oriental clinics in the neighborhood?
嗯…不錯的主意！你知道附近有中醫診所嗎？

Tae

In fact, I do! I'll text u the number.
其實，我知道！我傳電話號碼給你。

Jas

Great, thx.
太好了，謝啦。

Tae

My mom used to go there. Says it's great.
我媽媽常去那裡，她說不錯。

Jas

Yeah? That's good to know.
是嗎？太好了。

🔖 back to normal: 回到正常、好轉　　　Tae

Give them a call. You'll be back to normal in no time.
打電話給他們。你會馬上好轉的。

More to Talk!

與中醫有關的句子

My doctor gave me a mixture of herbs to take for weight loss. 我的醫生給我一包減肥用的中藥。

Ginseng is good for people who have cold feet and hands. 人蔘對手腳冰冷的人很有用。

When all the other treatments failed I turned to traditional medicine for a cure. 當所有的治療法都失敗，我轉向傳統醫療。

I prefer holistic forms of healing to modern Western medicine. 我偏好整合性的治療勝於現在西醫。

p 100

ChitChat **038**

Speak for yourself.

No offense 無意冒犯
addict 上癮者
Speak for yourself. 那是你自己的看法。
Same here. 我也是。
speaking of which 說到這個
born ready 完全準備好了

p 102

ChitChat **039**

He lives off ramen and soda.

senior citizen 老人
He lives off Instant noodles and soda.
他靠泡麵和汽水維生。
fatigue 疲勞

p 104

ChitChat **040**

What exactly is that?

vegan 純素主義者
What exactly is that? 那個究竟是什麼？
vegetarian 素食主義者
kudos 讚嘆
limited 被限制的
seafood 海鮮
unprocessed food 未加工過的食物
additives 添加物

p 106

ChitChat **041**

I'm not sure what she's into.

(I'm) Not sure what she's into. 我不確定
她喜歡什麼。
trendy 流行的、最近受歡迎的
frozen 冷凍的

p 108

ChitChat **042**

What should I eat to up my stamina?

Tell me about it. 可不是嗎？
What should I eat to up my stamina?
我該吃什麼來增強體力？
eel 鰻魚
have a strong stomach 有個強健的胃
~ will do ～ 就可以
usual spot 老地方

p 110

ChitChat **043**

I occasionally splurge on weekends.

tempted 被誘惑的
lose a ton of weight 瘦很多
get hooked on 迷上 ~
yo-yo effect 溜溜球效應

ChitChat 044 p 112

The meat was dry and the veggies were all mushy.

The meat was dry and the veggies were all mushy. 肉很乾，蔬菜也太軟爛了。
veggies vegetables 的簡稱
place 餐廳、商店、家
have a craving for ~ 非常想吃 ~
scrumptious 超級好吃的
yummy 好吃的

ChitChat 045 p 114

Do they have any lo-cal options?

(It) depends. 不一定
Do they have any lo-cal options? 他們有低卡路里食物嗎？
count calories 計算卡路里
artificial sweetener 代糖

ChitChat 046 p 116

My stomach is growling.

My stomach is growling. 我的胃在咕嚕咕嚕叫。
come to think of it 這樣一想
order in 點餐、叫外送
appetite 胃口
quench 解渴
thirst 口渴
hunger 飢餓

ChitChat 047 p 118

What are you in the mood for?

What are you in the mood for? 妳想吃什麼？
avoid 避免
carbs(carbohydrates) 碳水化合物
caught in traffic 塞車
bumper-to-bumper 車水馬龍

ChitChat 048 p 120

You're hitting the gym pretty hard.

You're hitting the gym pretty hard. 你很勤跑健身房。
I hear you. 我知道了。
weight training 重量訓練
cardio 有氧運動
circuit training 循環訓練
do weight training 做重量訓練
do cardio 做有氧運動

ChitChat 049 p 122

My head is killing me.

My head is killing me. 我的頭痛死了。
flu 流行性感冒
go around 流行
porridge 粥
last minute 最後一刻
OTC drugs(Over The Counter drugs) 不需處方箋的藥

come down with a cold 感冒

ChitChat 050 p 124
I'm quitting alcohol cold turkey!

hangover 宿醉
sleep the hangover off 用睡眠來解宿醉
I'm quitting alcohol cold turkey. 我要戒酒。
Easier said than done. 說的比做容易。
dog hair remedy 解宿醉的方法

ChitChat 051 p 126
I tripped while texting and walking.

sprain 扭傷
I tripped while texting and walking. 我走路打字時絆倒了。
swollen 腫的
black and blue 瘀腫的
twist one's ankle 扭傷腳踝
throw one's back out 閃到腰

ChitChat 052 p 128
My head feels foggy.

panic attack 恐慌症
foggy 模糊的
My head feels foggy. 我覺得意識模糊。
nauseous 噁心
dizzy 頭暈

ChitChat 053 p 130
Worry can make you sick.

workaholic 工作狂
prescription 處方箋
take a few days off work 休息幾天
Worry can make you sick. 憂慮會讓你生病。
relieve some stress 減輕壓力

ChitChat 054 p 132
I'll keep my fingers crossed.

deathly 非常、嚴重地
cavity 蛀牙
leave someone hanging 把～晾在一旁
I'll keep my fingers crossed. 我會為你祈禱。

ChitChat 055 p 134
You'll be back to normal in no time.

take its toll 造成損失
acupuncture 針灸
Oriental clinic 中醫診所
You'll be back to normal in no time. 你會馬上好轉的。
holistic forms of healing 整合醫學（不只重視身體，連精神面也一併治療的綜合方法）

CHAT

05

Relationships
人際關係

She's driving me up the wall. 我被她氣瘋了。

電玩宅

♪outta: out of 的口語

Get me outta this house.
把我弄出這間房子。

♪prob: problem，問題　　Bean

What's the prob now?
又有什麼問題？

電玩宅

♪drive someone up the wall: 被 ~ 氣瘋

It's my mom again. She's driving me up the wall.
又是我媽媽，我被她氣瘋了。

Bean

She just wants you to get a job.
她只是想要你找工作。

電玩宅

♪hounding: 折磨

Well it's not that easy!
And her hounding me certainly isn't helping.
這不是那麼容易！她折磨我完全沒有幫助。

Bean

She just needs to see that ur trying.
她只是想看到你嘗試。

電玩宅

> **I AM trying. Why can't she just trust me?**
> 我正在試。為何她不相信我就好？

🎵 U'll: you'lll 的網路用語   Bean

> **Keep searching. U'll find something soon.**
> 繼續找，你馬上就會找到的。

電玩宅

> **Let's hope.**
> 希望如此。

🎵 in the meantime: 這段期間   Bean

> **In the meantime, just ignore her nagging.**
> **It's just her worrying about you.**
> 這段期間就忽略她的嘮叨，這只是她的擔心。

More to Talk!

 ## 與煩心有關的句子

Stop pestering me! 不要折騰我！

My little brother is really annoying. 我弟弟真的很煩人。

When I was younger the other kids teased me a lot. 我小時候，其他孩子經常取笑我。

It's really irritating when people don't use their headphones. 不使用耳機真的令人厭煩。

It drives me nuts that my boyfriend drinks so much. 男朋友喝太多令我快抓狂了。

I couldn't believe my eyes!
我不敢相信我的眼睛！

 小秘書

> You know Jean on the 5th floor?
> 你認識 5 樓的 Jean 嗎？

Kell2013

> That stuck up snob who never says hi to anybody first?
> 絕對不會先打招呼的那個勢利女？

 小秘書

> Yes.
> 對。

Kell2013

> What about her?
> 她怎麼了？

 小秘書

> I just bumped into her in the elevator. And guess what?
> 我剛在電梯碰見她了，猜猜怎麼了？

Kell2013

> What? Hurry up and spill.
> 怎麼了？趕快說。

 小秘書

> Like Hyun was in with me talking...
> 我和 Hyun 正在說話…

Kell2013

Oh, that hot shot lawyer Hyun?
噢，那個了不起的大律師 Hyun？

小秘書

🖉 jump into conversation: 插話

Yeah. And out of nowhere she jumped into our conversation.
嗯，然後她突然插入我們的對話。

🖉 hit on ~: 勾引、挑逗

Kell2013

Was she hitting on him?
她在勾引他？

小秘書

More than that. She was all over him.
不只那樣，她完全是緊貼上了。

🖉 He's out of her league.: 她配不上他。

Kell2013

Leave it alone. He's way out of her league anyway.
別管她，反正她配不上他。

小秘書

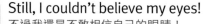

Still, I couldn't believe my eyes!
不過我還是不敢相信自己的眼睛！

 與個性有關的句子

He's only shy with me. He's normally super outgoing. 他只在我面前害羞，他平常是超級外向的。

She's a picky eater. 她很挑食。

He's narrow-minded and intolerant. 他內心狹隘又沒耐心。

I'm not a pushover. 我不是一個耳根子軟的人。

He's too stubborn to ever admit he's wrong. 他很固執，絕對不會承認自己的錯誤。

Just don't screw this up.

不要搞砸了。

 Tae

I got you that interview.
我幫你安排了面試。

電玩宅

🔗 You rock!: 你超強！

AWESOME! Thanks, man! You rock!
太棒了！謝謝你，朋友！你超強！

 Tae

🔗 ur: you're 的網路用語

I know. Haha. But it doesn't mean ur getting the job.
我知道，呵呵。不過那不代表你找到工作了。

電玩宅

I know. I know.
我知道，我知道。

 Tae

🔗 @ 4: at 4 的網路用語 / Was=(It) was

It's Monday @ 4.
Was the only opening as Jas is leaving town that night.
星期一 4 點。Jas 那天晚上要走，只有那時有空。

電玩宅

Ok. Got it. Have a few things to do in the morning n I'm there.
OK，我知道了，早上做幾件事情後就過去。

Tae

Just don't screw this up.
I don't wanna look stupid in front of Jas.
不要搞砸了。我不想在 Jas 面前看起來蠢笨。

電玩宅

Don't worry! I'm not going to mess up my only chance.
別擔心！我不會搞砸我唯一的機會。

Tae

🔖 ya: you 的口語

Alright, buddy. Best of luck to ya then.
好，朋友，祝你好運。

🔖 rat race: 激烈的生存競爭

電玩宅

Thx. Hopefully I'll be part of the rat race
next time we chat!
謝啦，希望下次我們聊天時我是這激烈競爭中
的一份子。

 與犯錯有關的句子

There isn't much you can do to make up for that kind of mistake. 你已經無法彌補那樣的錯誤。

I crashed and burned in my job interview. 我完全搞砸了工作面試。

Is it too late for me to fix the problem? 糾正這個問題已經太遲了嗎？

He only said that to save face after that callous remark. 在聽到那樣侮辱的言詞後，他那樣說只是為了保留面子。

You've got it all wrong.

你完全搞錯了。

 Kell2013 🖉hear through the grapevine: 傳聞、聽到小道消息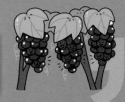

> I heard through the grapevine that you're in town.
> 我聽到小道消息說你在市區。

Jas

> Yeah, but I'm leaving tomorrow.
> 對，但我明天就走了。

 Kell2013

> What?! How long have you been here?
> 什麼？你在這裡待幾天了？

Jas

> For 5 days now.
> 今天是第 5 天。

 Kell2013

> And you didn't think to message me?
> 然後你沒想到傳訊息給我？

🖉You've got it all wrong.: 你完全搞錯了。 Jas

> But you've got it all wrong. I'm here to do interviews.
> 妳完全搞錯了，我來這裡是為了面試。

 Kell2013 🖉lunch or something: 吃個午餐什麼的

> Still, we could have grabbed lunch or something.
> 我們仍然可以吃個午餐什麼的。

✐hectic: 忙碌的、緊湊的

Jas

You know how hectic my schedule is.
妳知道我的日程有多緊湊。

Kell2013

Well how about tonight?
嗯，今晚如何？

Jas

I'm meeting some game designers tonight.
今晚我要和幾位遊戲設計師見面。

Kell2013

ALL night?
整個晚上？

✐tonite = tonight

Jas

How about meeting just for a drink tonite?
約喝一杯如何？

Kell2013   ✐I'll take what I can get.: 如果沒辦法，也只好這樣了。

I'll take what I can get.
如果沒辦法，也只好這樣了。

 ## 與固執有關的句子

Alright. If you insist, I'll take it. 好吧，如果你堅持，我會接受。

What should I do with this stubborn guy? 我該拿那個固執的男人怎麼辦？

Like father like son. You two are so obstinate. 有其父必有其子，你們都這麼固執。

My puppy is very headstrong and hard to train. 我的小狗非常任性，很難訓練。

Stop talking back to me! 不要再頂嘴了！

He's creeping me out.
他讓我渾身不舒服。

Bean　　🖉act weird: 行為怪異

He is acting really weird.
他的行為真的很奇怪。

小秘書

How so?
怎麼說？

Bean　　🖉status: 狀態消息

I dunno.. He just... Everywhere I go he's there.
And whenever I update my status he is the first to
comment. Always calling too.
我不知道⋯只是⋯我去的每個地方，他都在那裡，而且每次
我更新狀態消息時，他都是第一個回覆的，也老是打電話。

🖉What's the big deal?: 有什麼大不了的？　　小秘書

What's the big deal?
He's always online so he's the first to comment.
有什麼大不了的？他總是在線上，所以第一個回覆。

Bean　　🖉or sumthin: (or something 的網路用語) 諸如此類

He's creeping me out. U think he likes me or sumthin?
他讓我渾身不舒服，妳覺得他可能喜歡我嗎？

🖉paranoid: 被害妄想症 / awkward: 笨拙的　　小秘書

Stop being paranoid! He's just a little awkward is all.
別亂想了！他只是有點笨拙。

Bean

🖉*drink* coffee: drink 前面的 * 號表示強調。

He keeps asking me about different coffee blends. I'm pretty sure he doesn't even *drink* coffee.
他一直問我各種咖啡品牌的問題，我很確定他完全不喝咖啡。

小秘書

U really think there's somethin else going on?
妳真的覺得有點什麼嗎？

Bean

Not sure. Maybe it's nothing.
不確定，也許不是。

🖉bout =about / tell: 區分、分辨

小秘書

How bout I come by ur shop next time he's there? I'll be able to tell if he's being weird.
下次他在的話，我去妳店裡轉轉如何？我可以判斷他怪不怪。

Bean   🖉(I) was just about to ~.: 正要 ~

Was just about to suggest that!
我正想要這麼說！

 與別人有關的句子

He is acting kind of peculiar. 他的行為有點特別。

Everyone around me is acting really odd. 在我身邊的每個人都很奇怪。

It's unusual that my boss would call at that hour. 我老闆在這個時間打電話並不尋常。

People are saying a lot of strange things. 人們正在談論著許多奇怪的事情。

Something funny is going on but I have no idea what! 有什麼有趣的正在發生，但我不知道是什麼。

He's a total nightmare!

他完全是個惡夢！

 Bean

> Hey. U there? I think I'm gonna scream...
> 嘿，妳在嗎？我想要尖叫。

Kell2013

> What's up?
> 怎麼了？

 Bean

> Ugh. Where do I even begin...
> 我該從何說起…

Kell2013

> Uh-oh. Is this about your interview?
> 喔～跟妳的面試有關嗎？

 Bean

> I never told you? They gave the job to someone else!
> 我沒跟妳說嗎？他們把工作給了其他人了！

Kell2013

> I'm so sorry to hear that.
> 我很抱歉聽到這消息。

Bean

🖊 He's a micromanager.: 他管太多

Yeah... And the guy they gave it to acts like a drill sergeant. He is always yelling, rude to customers, and is a micromanager.

對⋯然後那個他們選的人就像個教育班長,他總是大呼小叫、對顧客無禮又管太多。

Kell2013

He sounds like a nightmare.

聽起來他是個惡夢!

Bean

He's a total nightmare! I'm already looking for another job.

他完全就是!我已經在找其他工作了。

Kell2013

Good idea. It's probably time to move on anyway.

妳想得對,似乎是時候另尋出路了。

 與遺憾有關的句子

You poor thing! 你真可憐!
That's too bad. 這太糟糕了!
That's a shame. 真可惜。
I can't believe it. 我不敢相信!
No way! 不可能!

More to Talk!

I'll make it up to you.

我會補償你的。

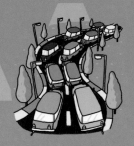

 Jas

It's 6. Where are you?
6 點了，妳在哪裡？

Kell2013

Running 30 minutes late.
我會慢個 30 分鐘。

 Jas

Not again!
又來了！

🔖make it up to: 補償 ~ Kell2013

I'll make it up to you!
我會補償你的。

 Jas

I'm getting pretty tired of always waiting for you.
我很厭煩總是要等妳。

🔖a ton of traffic: 塞車 Kell2013

Don't be mad, there's a ton of traffic.
不要生氣，路上塞車了。

 Jas 🔖put up with ~: 忍受 ~

I don't know why I put up with you anymore. >:O
我不知道為何我還要再忍受妳。

🖋come clean: 自首、招供

Kell2013

I'll come clean. I'm running late because I had to change.
我自首，我遲到是因為我必須換衣服。

Jas

Change? Why?
換衣服？為什麼？

Kell2013

I didn't want to go out wearing my work clothes.
我不想穿上班穿的衣服出去。

Jas

I should just go home!
我應該直接回家的！

🖋overdramatic: 反應過度的

Kell2013

Don't be so overdramatic.
I said I would make it up to you somehow.
不要反應過度了，我說我會補償你的。

Jas

Well, you had better make it good!
妳最好想個方法補償！

  與生氣有關的句子

Don't be angry at me. I'll explain. 不要生氣，我會解釋。
Stop pissing me off! 不要惹我！
He started getting on my nerves. 他開始惹毛我了。
He has a bad temper. 他脾氣不好。
My brother is hot-tempered. 我哥哥很火爆。

More to Talk!

Things aren't the same anymore. 現在跟以前不一樣了。

 電玩宅

> **U busy?**
> 忙嗎？

 電玩宅

> **Hello?**
> 哈囉？

Bean

> **Where r the guys these days?**
> 他們最近在哪裡？

 電玩宅

> **I dunno. Don't see much of them. Things aren't the same anymore.**
> 不知道，不常見到他們，現在跟以前不一樣了。

🖊 Y's that = Why is that

Bean

> **Y's that?**
> 為什麼？

 電玩宅

> **Not sure. I think they are avoiding each other. Or me. Who knows?**
> 不確定，我想他們正在躲對方，或者是躲我，誰知道？

Bean

> **That's too bad.**
> 真是太糟了。

電玩宅

✏ wanna go = Do you want to go / place: 商店、餐廳

So, wanna go to that noodle place I was telling you about?
妳想去我告訴過妳的那家麵店嗎？

Bean

Umm... hold on a sec.
嗯…等一下。

Bean

Yeah. Ok. Let's go.
嗯，OK，走吧！

電玩宅

Great. I'll pick you up in 10.
好的，10 分鐘後我去接妳。

✏ btw = by the way   Bean

Jamie is coming too btw.
順便說一下，潔米也會去。

電玩宅

K.
OK。

More to Talk!

 各種「不知道」的說法

Who knows? 誰知道？
How should I know? 我該知道嗎？
I wouldn't know. 我不知道。
No idea. 不知道。
I haven't the slightest idea. 我完全不知道。
Beats me! 不知道！

CHAT 05 **155**

Let me get back to you later.

我等一下回妳。

Kell2013

Got plans for tonight?
今晚有約嗎？

hubby = husband 老公　　　安琪兒

I think I'm gonna stay in with my hubby.
我想我會和老公在家。

Kell2013

Just bring him out too.
那也帶他來。

安琪兒

Why? What's going on?
為什麼？有什麼事嗎？

Kell2013

There's a new restaurant opening. It should be fun.
開了一家新餐廳，應該會很有趣。

安琪兒

My husband is being really lazy today.
我老公今天真的很懶。

Kell2013

That's not news. He's always lazy.
這不是新聞，他總是很懶。

安琪兒

**He's just been sitting around all day,
I don't even think he showered.**
他整天一直發懶，好像連澡都不想洗。

Kell2013

✎TMI = Too Much Information 不想知道太詳細

Gross!!! TMI.
好噁！！我不想知道太詳細。

安琪兒

Wait. Let me get back to you later.
等一下，我等一下回妳。

Kell2013

Don't be too late, I need to make reservations!
不要太晚，我得預約！

💡 與個人衛生有關的句子

Wash your hands as soon as you get home. 一回到家就要洗手。

Cleansing wipes are convenient for taking makeup off. 卸妝用卸妝棉很方便。

Using deodorant is a must in the summer. 夏天使用體香劑是必須的。

Wearing damp socks is bad for you. You may get athlete's foot. 穿濕襪子對你不好，你可能會得到香港腳。

Stop picking your nose! 不要再挖鼻孔！

Your heart was in the right place. 你的用意是好的。

 天鵝

> I feel so lousy.
> 我覺得心情很糟。

小秘書

🖉 Boo: 親愛的 (對熟人的稱呼)

> What's the matter, Boo?
> 怎麼了，親愛的？

 天鵝

> Where do I even start? Ugh. So apparently that guy I went on a few dates w/ is King_Michael's friend.
> 我要從哪裡說起？嗯，顯然是關於那個和我約了幾次會的人，原來他是 King_Michael 的朋友。

小秘書

> No way! How'd you find out?
> 怎麼會！妳怎麼知道的？

 天鵝

🖉 turn white: 臉色變白、嚇一跳

> We ran into him on our way to dinner!
> When he saw us together his face turned white.
> 我們去吃晚餐時在路上遇見他了！他看到我們在一起，臉色都白了。

小秘書

> Oh my god. Did you say anything?
> 天啊！妳有說什麼嗎？

天鵝

🖊 n: and 的網路用語

I said hi and he pretended like he was really busy n left. I felt so bad I called him later that night to say sorry for everything.
我打招呼，但他假裝很忙碌就離開了。我感覺很糟，所以之後晚上打電話給他為所有的事抱歉。

小秘書

You didn't have to do that. You didn't do anything wrong!
妳不用這樣做的，妳沒做錯事！

 天鵝

🖊 smooth things over: 平息、圓滿解決

He freaked out on me for calling. I just wanted to apologize and maybe smooth things over.
他被我的電話激怒，我只是想道歉，讓事情圓滿解決。

🖊 rly = really 真的

小秘書

Your heart was in the right place but u rly shouldn't have called him.
妳的用意是好的，但妳真的不用打電話給他。

天鵝 🖊 now I know: 現在我知道了

Now I know.
現在我知道了。

 與偶然有關的句子

What a coincidence it is to see you here! 在這裡遇到你真是太巧了！

He just appeared out of nowhere. 他不知道從哪兒冒出來。

I turned around and guess who was there! 我轉過身後，猜猜看誰在那裡！

I bumped into her on my way to work. 去公司的路上我偶然遇見她了。

I looked up and saw my old roommate standing in front of me. 我抬頭一看，看到我前室友站在我面前。

We have a love-hate relationship. 我們是又愛又恨的關係。

小秘書
> Bean is so annoying!
> Bean 令人討厭！

🖉 get along: 和睦相處、處得來　　　　　　　天鵝

> Uh-oh are you two fighting again? Why can't you just get along?!
> 你們兩個又吵架了嗎？為什麼妳們就不能好好相處？

小秘書
> Ask her. She's the reason we fight.
> 妳問她，她是我們吵架的原因。

天鵝

> Yeah yeah. You say that now but last week you two were doing everything together. Are you going to cancel on the Busan trip?
> 是，是，妳現在這樣說，但上星期妳們兩個才做什麼事都黏在一起。妳要取消釜山旅行嗎？

小秘書
> Me? Why should I?
> 我？為什麼我要取消？

天鵝

🖉 bicker: 拌嘴

> Well if you two are fighting then one of you should. I'm not listening to bickering the entire weekend.
> 如果妳們正在吵架，妳們其中一個就該這樣做。我不想整個周末都在聽妳們拌嘴。

小秘書

It's not that bad... And if anyone cancels it should be her!
沒那麼糟⋯而且如果有人該取消的話，應該是她！

天鵝

🔊 unbearable: 不能忍受的

When you two fight it's unbearable for the rest of us.
當妳們兩個吵架，我們其他人都很不能忍受。

小秘書

We'll be fine I promise. More than fine actually!
We're going to have so much fun!
我答應妳我們會和好的，而且事實上會更好！旅行會很好玩的！

天鵝

So now you're okay with her?
所以現在妳和她和好了？

小秘書

What can I say? We have a love-hate relationship.
我能說啥？我們是又愛又恨的關係。

More to Talk!

 與吵架有關的句子

Is it really worth getting upset over? 這個真的值得難過嗎？

I hate when people argue over such trivial things. 我討厭為了這種瑣事和人吵架。

As mad as you are it's still not okay to raise your voice. 無論你有多生氣，提高音量仍然是不好的。

The lady in the drama got so mad she threw a glass of water in her boyfriend's face. 電視劇裡的女生生氣到把杯子裡的水潑到男友臉上。

He started cursing at me so I just hung up. 他開始咒罵我，所以我就掛掉電話了。

ChitChat **056**   p 140

She's driving me up the wall.

Get me out. 把我弄出來。

prob. problem 的縮寫

What's the prob? 有什麼問題？

She's driving me up the wall. 我被她氣瘋了。

hounding 折磨

helping 有幫助的

Let's hope. 希望如此。

in the meantime 同時、這段期間

nagging 嘮叨

ignore one's nagging 忽視 ~ 的嘮叨

pester 折騰、為難

Stop pestering me. 不要折騰我！

annoying 令人厭煩的

tease 取笑

drive someone nuts 令 ~ 抓狂

ChitChat **057**   p 142

I couldn't believe my eyes!

stuck up snob 勢利的人

bump into 碰見

hot-shot 很有前途的、很厲害的

out of nowhere 突然

jump into one's conversation 插入 ~ 的對話

hit on ~ 勾引

More than that. 不只那樣

all over ~ 挑逗 ~

out of one's league 比 ~ 水準高的

I couldn't believe my eyes. 我不敢相信我的眼睛。

super outgoing 超級外向

picky eater 挑食的人

narrow-minded 心胸狹隘

intolerant 沒耐心

pushover 耳根子軟的人

stubborn 固執

admit 承認

ChitChat **058**   p 144

Just don't screw this up.

You rock! 你超強！

the only opening 唯一有空的時間

opening 空閒時間

Got it! 我知道了！

Just don't screw this up. 別搞砸了。

mess up 搞砸

buddy 朋友

hopefully 希望

rat race 激烈的生存競爭

make up for ~ 彌補 ~

crash and burn 完全搞砸

fix the problem 糾正問題

save face 保留面子

callous remark 侮辱性的言詞

ChitChat **059**   p 146

You've got it all wrong.

hear through the grapevine　傳聞、聽到
小道消息
message　傳訊息
You've got it all wrong.　你完全搞錯了。
grab lunch　吃個午餐
hectic　忙碌的
I'll take what I can get.　如果沒辦法，也只
好這樣了。
if you insist　如果你堅持
Like father like son.　有其父必有其子。
obstinate　固執的
headstrong　任性的
Stop talking back to me.　不要再頂嘴了！

ChitChat **060**   p 148

He's creeping me out.

weird　奇怪的
act weird　行為奇怪的
status　狀態、消息
update one's status　更新 ~ 的狀態消息
What's the big deal?　有什麼大不了的？
creep someone out　讓 ~ 渾身不舒服
He's creeping me out.　他讓我渾身不舒
服。
paranoid　被害妄想症
Stop being paranoid!　別再亂想了！
awkward　笨拙的
be about to~　正要 ~

eccentricity　反常
peculiar　特別的
act odd　行為怪異

ChitChat **061**   p 150

He's a total nightmare!

drill sergeant　教育班長
yell　大呼小叫
rude　無禮的
micromanager　管太多的人
He's a total nightmare.　他完全是個惡夢。
You poor thing!　你真可憐！
That's a shame!　真可惜！
No way!　不可能！

ChitChat **062**   p 152

I'll make it up to you.

Not again!　又來了！
I'll make it up to you.　我會補償你的。
get tired of ~　對 ~ 感到厭倦
a ton of traffic　塞車
put up with　忍受
come clean　自首、招供
run late　遲到
work clothes　上班穿的衣服
overdramatic　反應過度的
somehow　以某種方式
Stop pissing me off!　不要惹我！
get on one's nerves　惹毛
have a bad temper　壞脾氣

hot-tempered 火爆的

ChitChat **063** p 154

Things aren't the same anymore.

Things aren't the same anymore. 現在跟以前不一樣了。
avoid each other 互相躲對方
Who knows? 誰知道？
noodle place 麵店
hold a sec 等一下
pick someone up 接 ~

ChitChat **064** p 156

Let me get back to you later.

stay in with someone 和 ~ 在家
hubby 丈夫
bring someone out 帶 ~ 出來
sit around 發懶、閒晃
gross 噁心的
Let me get back to you later. 我等一下回你。
cleansing wipes 卸妝棉
take makeup off 卸妝
deodorant 體香劑、除臭劑
damp 濕的
athlete's foot 香港腳、足癬
pick one's nose 挖鼻孔

ChitChat **065** p 158

Your heart was in the right place.

lousy 心情不好的、可怕的
boo 親愛的
on one's way to ~ 在 ~ 的路上
turn white 臉色變白、嚇一跳
pretend 假裝 ~
freak out 激怒、吃驚
smooth ~over 圓滿解決、平息
Your heart was in the right place. 妳的用意是好的。
Now I know. 現在我知道了。
coincidence 巧合

ChitChat **066** p 160

We have a love-hate relationship.

get along 和睦相處、處得來
cancel 取消
Why should I? 為什麼我得要？
bicker 拌嘴
unbearable 不能忍受的
We have a love-hate relationship. 我們是又愛又恨的關係。
argue 吵架
trivial 細微的
raise one's voice 提高音量
curse 咒罵

CHAT

06

Tech
科技

My contract is up.
我的合約到期了。

Bean

Need your opinion about a phone.
我需要你提供有關手機的意見。

電玩宅

You've come to the right guy! What's up?
妳找對人了！怎麼回事？

Bean

Which is better, Apple or Samsung?
蘋果和三星哪一個比較好？？

🔖 depend on ~: 依據 ~、取決於 ~ 　　電玩宅

It depends on the phone really. Why?
這要看是哪種手機，怎麼了？

Bean

My contract is up. I'm not sure if
I should switch providers either.
我的合約到期了，我也不確定是否我應該換電信公司。

🔖 (phone) service plan: 月租費服務　　電玩宅

I'm pretty happy with mine. How much data comes with your
service plan?
我很滿意我的。妳的月租費可用多少流量？

Bean

2GB. And I get 500 minutes.
2GB，還有 500 分鐘免費。

電玩宅

For how much?
這樣多少？

Bean

90,000 won.
9 萬韓圜。

🎵rip off: 敲竹槓　　電玩宅

What a rip off!
妳被敲竹槓了！

Bean　　　　　　　　　　🎵cell phone: 手機

Ah... I thought it might be.
U think you could come cell phone shopping with me?
啊…我想有可能。你可以和我一起去手機店嗎？

電玩宅

It'd be my pleasure.
這是我的榮幸

📖 與手機有關的句子

I lost the charger and have to get a new one. 我弄丟了充電器，必須買一個新的。

You can get a prepaid phone at the airport when you arrive. 你到達後可以在機場買一支預付卡電話。

ABC Mobile is now offering family plans. ABC 電信現在提供家庭月租費計畫。

They have rollover minutes so it's not a big deal if they use too much airtime. 剩下的通話時間可轉到下個月，所以講太多電話也沒關係。

My phone doesn't have a good signal. 我的手機訊號不好。

Just give it a go! 放心試試看！

Kell2013

Help!!! I have Trojan viruses on my laptop.
幫幫忙！我的筆電中了特洛伊木馬病毒。

🔖 get rid of ~: 清除

小秘書

Then get rid of them. U know how, right?
刪除它們。妳知道方法，對吧？

Kell2013

Told you I know nothing about computers.
我告訴過妳我完全不懂電腦。

小秘書

Just give it a go.
放心試試看吧！

Kell2013　🔖 okey-doke: ok 的另一種拼法，我知道了，okey-dokey

Okey-doke.
我知道了。

Kell2013

I'm ready now. How?
我現在準備好了，要怎麼做？

小秘書

Delete the entire browsing history first.
首先把瀏覽紀錄全部刪掉。

Kell2013　🔖 I'm on it: 我照做了

Um... I'm on it.
嗯⋯我照做了。

小秘書

If you can't remove it all, follow the file location and delete the "temporary internet files".

如果妳無法完全清除，找到檔案位置，刪除網路暫存檔。

Kell2013

Ugh. It won't work.

啊…不行。

🔖 installation: 安裝

小秘書

Then you're gonna have to use an installation disk to reinstall Windows.

那麼妳必須使用安裝磁片重新安裝 Windows。

Kell2013

Ahhhh, it's getting more complicated.

呃，愈來愈複雜了。

小秘書

Don't forget to back up your data before formatting your computer.

在格式化妳的電腦之前，別忘了把資料備份。

Kell2013

I won't.

我不會忘的。

More to Talk!

 ## 與電腦有關的句子

My nephew is computer savvy. 我姪子是電腦專家。

Computers age fast. 電腦很快就過時了。

How do I hook this phone up to my computer? 我要怎麼把這個手機與電腦連結？

Have you ever had your computer turn off w/o warning? 你曾遇過電腦沒有警告就自動關機嗎？

Tell me how I can install this software on my computer. 告訴我如何在我的電腦上安裝這個軟體。

I'm having trouble figuring this thing out. 我在解決這個問題時遇到麻煩。

Bean

🔖 have trouble -ing: 在 ~ 遇到麻煩

I'm having trouble figuring this thing out.
我在解決這個事情時遇到麻煩。

天鵝

Which thing?
什麼事？

Bean

🔖 tech-savvy: 科技專家

This tablet I bought for my aunt. Are you tech-savvy?
關於我買給姑姑的平板電腦。妳是技術方面的專家嗎？

天鵝

Somewhat. What's the problem?
懂一點。是什麼問題？

Bean

🔖 n stuff: and stuff 的簡稱，諸如此類的

I wanna get it set up with programs n stuff before
I give it to her but not sure how to download'em.
在我給姑姑之前，我想先安裝好軟體之類的，但我不知道要怎麼下載。

天鵝

You need an account.
妳需要一個帳號。

Bean

Ah, do I have to use my credit card?
喔，我需要使用信用卡嗎？

天鵝

I think if you want any paid apps. You should also set it up with your info instead.
如果妳想要付費的軟體就需要。妳也應該用妳的資料設定。

Bean

Why's that?
為什麼要那樣？

📎ruin the surprise: 毀掉驚喜　　　　天鵝

She might get an email about the account and it'd ruin the surprise.
她可能會收到關於帳號的電子郵件，這樣就沒有驚喜了。

Bean　　　📎thinkin': thinking

OH good thinkin'. What kind of apps do you think a 50-year-old would like?
喔，好主意。妳覺得 50 歲的人會喜歡哪種軟體？

 📎You know: 你知道的　　　天鵝

Hmm. Something for photos, another for organization, maybe one for recipes. You know, the basics.
嗯，類似像照片、行程管理、或是食譜，妳知道的，基本的。

More to Talk!

🔦 與電腦有關的句子 2

I installed a few plugins on my browser to make my workflow more efficient. 我在瀏覽器上安裝了一些外掛程式，使我的工作流程更有效率。

You're running the outdated version. 你用的是舊版本。

If you enter the password incorrectly 3 times it locks. 如果你輸入 3 次錯誤的密碼，就會鎖住。

You need to install the updates first. 你需要先安裝更新的項目。

When you download a torrent you should scan it for viruses. 你下載種子檔案（註：副檔名為 .torrent 的檔案）時，你應該掃描有沒有病毒。

This is my last resort.
這是我最後的手段。

 電玩宅 ✏YT: You there 的簡稱，你在嗎？

Hey, YT?
嗨，在嗎？

Bean

Can't talk. Having a life crisis!
不能聊，出現人生的危機！

 電玩宅

What's wrong?
怎麼了？

Bean

My hard drive just crashed and I can't retrieve my files.
我的硬碟壞了，我無法復原我的檔案。

 電玩宅

Didn't you back them up?
妳沒備份嗎？

Bean

NO, that's why it's a life crisis!
沒有，所以才是我人生的危機！

🎧This is my last resort.: 這是我最後的手段。　　　　　　　　　Bean

> I'm about to go to the service center. This is my last resort!
> 我要去服務中心，這是我最後的方法。

電玩宅

> Doesn't your computer automatically back up on a cloud?
> 妳的電腦沒有自動備份到雲端嗎？

Bean

> Cloud?
> 雲端？

電玩宅

> Yeah, your files should be there.
> 對，妳的檔案應該會在那裡。

Bean

> How do I get it from a cloud?
> 我要怎麼從雲端上取得？

電玩宅　　🎧ring you: 打電話給妳

> I'll ring you and explain!
> 我打電話解釋給妳聽。

 ## 與電腦有關的句子 3

Help me with formatting my computer. 幫我格式化我的電腦。

What now? My computer froze. 現在要怎樣？我的電腦當機了。

My computer is running slower than usual. 我的電腦跑得比平常慢。

Your computer screen seems blurry. 你的電腦螢幕好像不清楚。

Help! My computer monitor's blinking on and off. 幫幫忙！我的電腦螢幕在閃爍。

It's gonna blow your mind!

你會大吃一驚的！

 King_Michael

> **Guess who's the new owner of a brand new convertible.**
> 猜猜看誰是這台新上市的敞篷車主人？

Tae

> **I think I can guess...**
> 我想我猜得到…

 King_Michael

> **It's a Beamer too.**
> 而且是 BMW。
>
>

Tae

> **Nice.**
> 不錯呢。

 King_Michael

✍ fully loaded: 具備了所有的配備選項

> **It's fully loaded. And it has a hard top that opens and closes automatically.**
> 這是全配，還有全自動開關的硬頂敞篷。

Tae

> **Sweet.**
> 好帥。

King_Michael

✐top of the line: 最高級的、最新型的

The sound system is top of the line, too. You'll see this weekend. It's gonna blow your mind!
音響系統也是最高級的，周末你就可以看到，你會大吃一驚的！

Tae

I bet it will. Having money must be nice, bro.
一定會的。有錢真好，朋友。

King_Michael

It sure is.
真的是這樣。

Tae

Lol
呵呵。

King_Michael

Don't worry, I'll be sure to take you around town in it.
別擔心，我一定會載你在市區繞繞。

Tae

You'd better!
一定要啊！

More to Talk!

 與開車有關的句子

Before getting your license you have to attend a driving school. 在你拿到駕照之前，你必須去駕訓班上課。

Always check your tires before a long road trip. 在長途開車之前總是要檢查你的輪胎。

My car is in the shop till Saturday. 我的車子在星期六之前都在汽車中心。

Children must always buckle their safety belts and babies must ride in car seats. 孩子們必須繫安全帶，而嬰兒必須坐汽車座椅。

Don't be a backseat driver! 開車時不要在旁邊指手畫腳。

It's revolutionized my life!
它徹底改變了我的人生！

 安琪兒

Our new kimchi refrigerator finally came!
我們的新泡菜冰箱終於來了！

Congrats: Congratulations 的簡稱　　Kell2013

Congrats! How do you like it?
恭喜！妳覺得如何呢？

 安琪兒

It's SO convenient. Now all the other food doesn't smell like kimchi.
太 ~~ 方便了，現在其他所有的食物都沒有泡菜味道了。

Kell2013

Lol
呵呵。

 安琪兒

I'm so psyched!!!!!!!
我太高興了！！！

Kell2013

Haha Calm down! It's just a fridge.
哈哈，冷靜點！這只是個冰箱。

安琪兒

JUST a fridge? It's revolutionized my life!
Think I might order a blender next.
「只是」個冰箱？ 它徹底改變了我的人生！下一個我可能會訂購攪拌機。

Kell2013

So how about you invite me over for dinner so I can see it?
所以妳什麼時候要邀請我吃晚餐，讓我看看？

安琪兒

be about to ~: 正要 ~

OMG I was just about to! How's Friday for you?
唉呦，我正要這樣說！星期五如何？

hectic: 忙碌的、緊湊的

Kell2013

Things are really hectic at the office.
The weekend is better. Sunday?
公司非常忙，週末比較好，星期日呢？

安琪兒

Sunday it is!
星期日吧！

More to Talk!

與泡菜有關的句子

There are several varieties but the most common type is cabbage kimchi.
泡菜有好幾種，但最常見的是白菜泡菜。

Fermented foods are good for health. 發酵食物對健康很好。

I love the spicy, pungent taste of cooked kimchi. 我喜歡味道強烈辛辣的熟泡菜。

This kimchi recipe has been passed down from generation to generation.
泡菜食譜是代代流傳下來的。

It's delicious but inconvenient to store. 這個雖然好吃，但保存不易。

It keeps turning off.
它一直關掉。

King_Michael

🎵 heat exhaustion: 中暑

I'm going to die from heat exhaustion.
我快中暑而死了。

電玩宅

LOL What's going on?
呵呵，怎麼了？

King_Michael

My air conditioner. It keeps turning off.
我的冷氣機，一直關掉。

電玩宅

Call the manufacturer. They'll send someone out to fix it.
打電話給廠商，他們會派人來修理。

King_Michael

I did. It's too old to be covered under warranty.
我打了，冷氣機太舊，無法保證可復原。

電玩宅

Did they say about how much they would charge?
他們有說要收多少錢嗎？

King_Michael

🎵 ain't: be/have 動詞的否定形 (非正式文法)

They said it ain't gonna be cheap and they can't send anyone for a week.
他們說不便宜，而且他們在這個星期內無法派人來。

✎ repairman: 維修人員、技師

電玩宅

Why not try calling a repairman? Jas was pretty happy with the one he used.
何不打電話給維修人員試試？Jas 很滿意他用過的人。

 King_Michael

I don't feel like spending the money.
我不想把錢花在這上面。

電玩宅

It's going to be one hot summer for you!
這對你會是一個非常熱的夏天。

 King_Michael

Yeah. Maybe I'll just buy a new one...
嗯，也許我乾脆買一個新的…

電玩宅

So much for not wanting to spend the money.
你不是才說不想花錢。

 King_Michael

What can I say, I prefer new electronics!
我能說啥，我更喜歡新的電子產品。

 ## 與 A/S 有關的句子

You should take it to the service center for repair. 你應該帶去服務中心修理。

The repairs cost more than the actual product! 修理費比實際的產品價格更高！

Water damage is not covered under the warranty. 因浸水造成的損害不在保固範圍裡。

Insurance for small electronics seems like a waste of money. 小型電子產品的保險似乎是浪費錢。

Can you recommend a good repair shop? 你可以介紹不錯的維修店嗎？

I shrank my entire wardrobe.

我整個衣櫃都縮水了。

小秘書

> My washing machine is a piece of garbage.
> 我的洗衣機完全是個垃圾。

天鵝

> LOL
> 呵呵

小秘書　　　　　　　　　　🖊 shrink: 收縮、縮小

> It's not funny. All my clothes are ruined!
> 一點也不好笑，我所有的衣服都毀了。

🖊 or something: 之類的　　　　天鵝

> Did the washer rust or something?
> 會是洗衣機生鏽之類的嗎？

小秘書　　　　　　　　　　🖊 malfunction: 故障

> No. I clearly hit "normal wash" and it malfunctioned and somehow used hot water.
> 不是，我明明按了「一般洗程」，然後就故障了，不知怎麼地用了熱水洗。

🖊 Oh man.: 狼狽、驚訝時的口頭語。　天鵝

> Oh man.
> 哎呀。

小秘書

I shrank my entire wardrobe.
我整個衣櫃都縮水了。

天鵝

So what are you going to do?
所以妳要怎麼做？

小秘書

🖉I feel like suing.: 我有想提告的心情。

I don't know but I feel like suing the manufacturer!
我不知道，但我想跟廠商提出告訴！

天鵝

That sounds rational. :P
聽起來有道理 (吐舌)~

小秘書

🖉roomie: roommate 的簡稱，室友

Until I figure this out I guess I'll have to wear my roomie's clothes. >:/
直到這件事解決之前，我都得穿室友的衣服了。

More to Talk!

 與家電有關的句子

The icemaker on the fridge is broken. 冰箱裡的製冰機壞掉了。

Hot water won't come out of the water cooler unless it's plugged in.
除非插頭插上，不然飲水機裡沒有熱水。

The vacuum still functions but has poor suction. 真空吸塵器仍然可以運作，但吸力很弱。

Don't forget to clean the filter every few weeks! 別忘了每隔幾個禮拜要清除濾網。

You need a dehumidifier in the summer and a humidifier in the winter.
你夏天需要除濕機、冬天需要加濕器。

I wish our house had a dishwasher. 我希望我們家有洗碗機。

Who can keep track of all these accessories?! 誰有辦法好好保管這所有的配件？

 Bean

> Ack! I think I left my charger at your place.
> 啊！我好像把我的充電器放在妳家了。

小秘書

> Really? I didn't see it.
> 真的嗎？我沒看到。

 Bean

> It's got to be there somewhere.
> My headphones aren't in my bag either!!
> 它應該會在某個地方。我的耳機也沒在我的包包裡。

🎙lying around: 到處亂放，四散各地　　小秘書

> I definitely didn't see any headphones lying around.
> 我確定沒看到什麼耳機亂放。

 Bean

> Oh well. My battery is too low. I can't listen to music anyway.
> 這樣喔。反正我電池也快沒電，沒辦法聽音樂。

小秘書

> I just bought new earphones myself. I'm always losing them.
> 我最近也買了新的耳機，我也老是弄丟它們。

 Bean　　🎙keep track of: 追蹤、掌握

> I know! Who can keep track of all these accessories?!
> 我知道！誰有辦法好好保管這所有的配件？

小秘書

Just don't replace yours with such expensive ones this time.
這次就不要換這麼貴的。

Bean

I'll be sure not to. Can you keep looking just in case they're there?
我一定不會。說不定它們在妳那邊，妳能幫忙找看看嗎？

小秘書

Will do. What color were they again?
我會的。妳再說一次是什麼顏色？

Bean

Hot pink.
亮粉色。

🔊 be on the lookout: 注意觀察、把風   小秘書

I'll be on the lookout!
我會注意看看的！

Bean

Thx.
謝謝。

 與電源有關的句子

Use my phone, it's fully charged. 用我的手機，它已經充飽電了。

Use a power strip instead of plugging directly into the wall to save power. 使用多頭插座代替直接插入插座，以節省電源。

This room doesn't have enough electric sockets. 這個房間的插座不夠多。

Ask the waiter if they can charge your phone while we eat. 問問看服務生是否可以在我們吃飯時幫忙充電手機。

My battery is running low. I'll have to switch it. 我的電池快沒電，必須換一個。

Can you charge it with this USB cable? 你可以用這條 USB 線充電嗎？

ChitChat 067 p 166

My contract is up.

come to the right guy 找對人了。
My contract is up. 我的合約到期了。
switch 變更
(service) provider 電信公司
service plan 合約、月租費計畫
What a rip off. 你被敲竹槓了。
cell phone 手機
charger 充電器
prepaid phone 預付卡電話
family plans 家庭月租費計畫
rollover 移轉
have a good signal 訊號很好

ChitChat 068 p 168

Just give it a go!

Trojan virus 特洛伊木馬病毒
Just give it a go! 放心試試看！
Okey-doke OK 的變形用語
browsing history 瀏覽紀錄
I'm on it. 我照做了。
temporary 暫時的
It won't work. 行不通。
installation 安裝
complicated 複雜的
format 格式化
computer savvy 電腦專家
hook up 連結

warning 警告

ChitChat 069 p 170

I'm having trouble figuring this thing out.

figure out 弄明白、解決
I'm having trouble figuring this thing out.
我在解決這個問題時遇到麻煩。
tech savvy 科技專家
somewhat 多少、一點
account 帳號
paid apps 付費軟體
ruin the surprise 毀掉驚喜
Good thinking. 好主意
recipe 食譜
basics 基本的東西
outdated version 舊版本
incorrectly 不正確地
scan 掃描

ChitChat 070 p 172

This is my last resort.

life crisis 人生的危機
hard drive 硬碟
crash 損壞
retrieve 取回
This is my last resort. 這是我最後的手段。

automatically 自動地
I'll ring you and explain. 我打電話解釋給
妳聽。
It froze up. 當機了。
blurry 模糊的
blinking 閃爍的

ChitChat 071 p 174
It's gonna blow your mind!

convertible 敞篷車
Beamer BMW
fully loaded 具備了所有的配備選項
Sweet! 好帥！
top of the line 最高級的
It's gonna blow your mind. 你會大吃一驚
的。
take someone around 帶～到處繞繞
shop 汽車中心
buckle 繫
safety belt 安全帶
Don't be a backseat driver. 開車時不要在
旁邊指手畫腳。

ChitChat 072 p 176
It's revolutionized my life!

kimchi refrigerator 泡菜冰箱
psyched 高興的
I'm so psyched! 我非常高興！

fridge 冰箱
revolutionize 改革、徹底改變
It's revolutionized my life. 它徹底改變了
我的人生。
cabbage 大白菜
fermented food 發酵食物
spicy 辣的
pungent 辛辣刺鼻的
recipe 食譜
pass down 代代相傳
from generation to generation 一代傳一
代
store 保存

ChitChat 073 p 178
It keeps turning off.

heat exhaustion 中暑
die from heat exhaustion 快中暑而死
air conditioner 冷氣機
It keeps turning off. 它一直關掉。
manufacturer 製造商
warranty 保固
repairman 維修人員
electronics 電子產品、家電
water damage 因浸水造成的損害
a waste of money 浪費錢
repair shop 維修店

ChitChat 074   p 180

I shrank my entire wardrobe.

shrink 收縮

I shrank my entire wardrobe. 我整個衣櫃都縮水了。

washer 洗衣機

rust 生鏽

or something. 之類的。

normal wash 一般洗程

malfunction 故障

sue 提告

I feel like suing. 我想提告。

figure out 弄清楚

ice maker 製冰機

water cooler 飲水機

vacuum 真空吸塵器

suction 吸入

clean the filter 清理濾網

Dehumidifier 除濕機

humidifier 加濕器

dish washer 洗碗機

ChitChat 075   p 182

Who can keep track of all these accessories?!

charger 充電器

lie around 到處亂放

keep track of ~ 追蹤、掌握

Who can keep track of all these accessories? 誰有辦法好好保管這所有的配件？

replace 替換

be on the lookout 把風

fully charged 完全充飽電

electric sockets 插座

CHAT

07

Leisure Activities

休閒活動

Bored out of my mind.

無聊死了。

 天鵝

What are you doing now?
妳現在在做什麼？

 Bean

Nothing. Bored out of my mind.
沒做什麼，無聊死了。

 天鵝

Me too! I'm sick of sitting in my room every weekend!
我也是！我受夠了每個週末都待在房間裡！

 Bean

Let's go somewhere! Wanna?
去哪裡逛逛！要嗎？

 天鵝

Right now?
現在？

 Bean

Why not? How about a picnic by the river? We can order chicken!
有何不可？去河邊野餐如何？我們可以點炸雞！

天鵝

I like the sound of that! Do you want to ride bikes?
我喜歡！妳想要騎腳踏車嗎？

Bean

Of course! I think my little brother left a kite here too.
當然好！我想我弟弟也有個風箏放在這裡。

天鵝

Wow! I haven't flown a kite since I was a kid!
哇！我長大以後就再也沒放過風箏了！

Bean

It's gonna be great!
這會很有趣的！

天鵝

Grab your sunglasses and meet me there!
戴著妳的太陽眼鏡在那裡見吧！

 ## 與休閒活動有關的句子

All the children gathered around to build a sand castle. 所有的孩子聚集起來堆沙堡。

If you don't like swimming you can always work on your tan. 如果你不喜歡游泳，那你也可以做日光浴。

There's nothing better than going to the ballpark with friends. 沒有什麼事情比和朋友們一起去棒球場更好的了。

Let's go to the soccer field and kick a ball around. 去足球場踢球吧！

If you go there in early spring you can catch the Cherry Blossom Festival. 如果你在早春時去那裡，你可以看到櫻花慶典。

We went on a double date to Everland. 我們兩對一起去愛寶樂園約會。

More to Talk!

I haven't gone anywhere in ages.

我好久沒去什麼地方了。

小秘書

R U going anywhere during the summer holidays?
妳暑假要去哪裡嗎？

🖉I can't afford it.: 我沒有那種閒暇時間。　Kell2013

You know I can't afford it. U?
妳知道我沒那種閒暇時間。妳呢？

小秘書　🖉sis: sister 的簡寫

Visiting my sis in LA.
要去拜訪住在 LA 的姊妹。

🖉BTW: by the way 的縮寫，順便一提　Kell2013

Nice. BTW, what's she doing there?
真好，不過她在那裡做什麼？

小秘書　🖉home making: 家事

Homemaking.
家務。

Kell2013

I see.
原來如此。

小秘書　🖉make time: 抽出時間、抽空

Make some time n come with me.
抽點時間和我一起去吧。

Kell2013

U know what my work is like.
妳知道我的工作是怎樣的。

小秘書　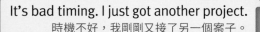 ✎work 24/7: 不分日夜、一週 24 小時一直工作

This is crazy. You can't work 24/7!!!
這太荒唐了，妳不可能一直工作。

 Kell2013

It's bad timing. I just got another project.
時機不好，我剛剛又接了另一個案子。

 小秘書

Alright.
好吧。

Kell2013

Maybe some other time.
也許下次有機會。

 小秘書

Freelancing doesn't mean you're free.
自由接案者不表示妳是自由的。

Kell2013

You tell me. I haven't gone anywhere in ages.
可不是？ 我好久沒去什麼地方了。

與聯絡有關的句子

More to Talk!

We'll see. 再看看。
Maybe next time. 也許下次。
See you in 20. 20 分鐘後見。
Can I take a rain check? 我可以留到下次嗎？
Call me. Don't be a stranger. 打電話給我，不要沒聯絡。

He's an athletic freak.

他是一個運動狂。

Kell2013

How was your date?
妳的約會如何？

小秘書

Don't even start.
別提了。

Kell2013

What's wrong?
怎麼了？

talk nonsense: 瞎扯淡　　小秘書

He kept talking nonsense...
他一直在瞎扯淡。

Kell2013

So he's humorous.
所以他很幽默。

小秘書

All he was talking was about giving workout advice.
他講的全部都是有關鍛鍊身體的建議。

Kell2013　well-informed: 見多識廣的

So he was well-informed.
所以他見多識廣。

workout freak: 運動狂、對運動執著的人　　小秘書

And the worst part is he was an athletic freak.
而且最糟的是他是個運動狂。

Kell2013   🖊 well-built: 健壯的

Oh, he must be well-built!!!
喔，他一定很健壯！！

小秘書

STOP!!! It's annoying.
夠了！！令人厭煩。

Kell2013

lol. Sooooory!
呵呵，抱抱抱抱歉！

🖊 rub it in: 在傷口撒鹽   小秘書

You don't have to rub it in.
妳不用在傷口撒鹽。

Kell2013

I said sorry.
我說抱歉了。

小秘書

...

Kell2013

Go for a beer? It's on me.
喝一杯啤酒？我請客。

More to Talk!

 ## 與運動有關的句子

There's nothing like running on the treadmill. 沒有什麼比得上在跑步機上跑步了。

Use the correct footwear to protect your joints. 穿著正確的鞋子以保護你的關節。

Yeah!!!! It was time well-spent in the gym. 耶！！在體育館的時間很充實。

Your trainer will help you set up the workout routine. 你的教練會幫你訂定訓練內容。

Stay hydrated during your workout. 運動時保持水份。

Most guys dream of having 6-pack abs. 大部份的男生都幻想有 6 塊腹肌。

I'm drawn to baking classes.

我對烘培課有興趣。

 Kell2013

Congrats! Now you're a certified barista.
恭喜！現在妳是認證過的咖啡師了。

 安琪兒

Thx. But I have mixed feelings.
謝謝，不過我的心情很複雜。

 Kell2013

Haven't you decided on what to do next?
妳無法決定下一步要做什麼？

nah: 不 (=no) 安琪兒

Nah.
嗯。

 Kell2013

I thought you wanted to open a coffee place.
我以為妳想要開一家咖啡店。

 安琪兒

That was my original plan, but I've changed my mind.
那是我原本的計畫，但我改變主意了。

 Kell2013

build up expertise: 累積專業知識

So, you want to build up coffee expertise working as a barista?
所以妳想要以咖啡師的身份工作來累積咖啡的專業知識？

🎵(I) can't picture ~: 無法想像

安琪兒

Can't picture myself working for someone else.
我無法想像我為某人工作。

Kell2013

What are you up to doing, then?
那麼妳打算要做什麼？

安琪兒
Well, running a bakery?
經營麵包店？

Kell2013
...

安琪兒
I'm drawn to baking classes lately.
我最近對烘培課感到興趣。

Kell2013
Uhmmm, at least you have some plans. Good.
嗯…至少妳有一些計畫，不錯。

More to Talk!

 ## 與職場有關的句子

He is a temp. 他是臨時性的。

Flexible working hours can't be guaranteed for 9-to-5ers. 朝九晚五的正職人員無法保證享有彈性工時。

Thanks to the five day work week system, he can have more quality time with his family. 感謝一週工作五天的制度，他可以和家人有更多的寶貴時光。

All temp workers long to be regular workers someday. 所有的臨時員工渴望某一天能成為正職員工。

CDF Mart hired 1,000 seasonal workers. CDF超市雇用了1000名季節性勞工。

Let's get together more often.
讓我們更常聚會吧！

 小秘書

Hey guys!
嘿 妳們！

Bean

Hi there.
嗨！

 小秘書 blast: 非常有趣的、興奮的

That was a blast!!!
太興奮了！！

天鵝

Same here. Fat burning n stress relief through working out...
我也是，我做運動來燃燒脂肪和消除壓力⋯

 小秘書

It's like killing two birds with one stone.
似乎是一石二鳥。

muscular: 肌肉的　　天鵝

And all the muscular guys in the gym...
而且健身房裡全都是肌肉男⋯

Bean

📎positive outlet: 正面的 (有益的) 出口、發洩手段

lol I know! Exercise sure is a positive outlet!
呵呵，沒錯！運動的確是正面的發洩出口！

📎on a regular basis: 規則性地、定期地

天鵝

lol Why don't we do this on a regular basis?
呵呵，我們何不定期運動呢？

小秘書

Good idea.
好主意。

Bean

Let's get together more often.
讓我們更常聚會吧。

天鵝

📎fit and healthy: 身體健康的

Working out is necessary to keep fit and healthy anyway.
無論如何要維持身體健康，健身是必須的。

📎Hear: 說得好　Bean

Hear! Hear!
說得好！說得好！

 與運動有關的句子 2

Let's hit the gym after work. 下班後去健身房吧！

Power walking burns more calories than running. 快走比跑步可燃燒更多卡路里。

You should stretch before and after a workout. 你應該在健身前後做伸展運動。

She has a very fast metabolism. 她的新陳代謝很快。

3 times per week is said to be ideal for strength training. 據說一週 3 次的肌力訓練是理想的。

It was a waste of time.
這是浪費時間。

 安琪兒　　　 ✎ ~stinks: 差勁、糟糕的

That movie stinks.
那部電影很差勁。

Kell2013

The 3D conversion?
那部 3D 版的？

安琪兒　　　 ✎ ridiculous 滑稽、荒唐的

I'm not a big fan of 3D movies, but this is ridiculous.
我沒有特別喜歡 3D 電影，但這個太荒唐了。

Kell2013

Did you see the original version?
妳看過原來的版本嗎？

 安琪兒

Sure. Who didn't?
當然，誰沒看過？

Kell2013

How many times did you see it?
妳看過幾次？

安琪兒

Twice in the cinema, several more times on DVD and cable.
電影院兩次，用 DVD 和有線電視看過好幾次。

🖉kill excitement: 使失去趣味 　　Kell2013

That must have killed the excitement of the remake?!
那重新製作的版本就一定沒意思了！

安琪兒　🖉It was a waste of time.: 我浪費時間了。

It was a waste of time, anyway.
反正這是浪費時間。

Kell2013

Sorry to hear that.
真是遺憾。

安琪兒　　　　　　　🖉take a nap: 小睡一下

I should have taken a nice long nap instead.
我應該在那時好好的睡一下才是。

 與電影有關的句子

What's on at the cinema? 這個電影院正在上映什麼電影？
What's the movie about? 那部電影的內容是什麼？
Who's it starring? 誰主演的？
Wanna get some popcorn? Salted or sweet? 想來點爆米花嗎？鹹的還是甜的？
Anything to drink? 要喝的嗎？

No wonder you're so good at English! 難怪妳的英文很好！

 天鵝

I hate practicing for English interviews!
我討厭練習英文面試。

🎵Wanna come to~ = Do you want to come to~ / convo = conversation　Bean

Wanna come to my English convo group?
想加入我的英文會話團體嗎？

 天鵝

English convo group?
英文會話團體？

Bean

We meet up twice a month and practice English over dinner and drinks.
我們一個月見面兩次，一邊吃晚餐喝飲料，一邊練習英文。

 天鵝

No wonder you're so good at English!
難怪妳的英文很好！

🎵give it a shot: 試一次看看 / simultaneously: 同時　Bean

You should give it a shot. You can make new friends, eat good food n study English simultaneously.
妳應該試一次。妳可以結交新朋友、吃好吃的食物，同時學習英文。

 天鵝　🎵be better off ~: ~ 會更好 / take classes: 上課

Maybe I'm better off taking classes.
There's a place near my house...
也許我上課會更好，我家附近有很多英語教室…

🖉ur: you're

Bean

We're currently accepting new members.
If ur interested let me know.
我們現在正在招募新成員，如果妳有興趣告訴我。

天鵝

🖉shy: 害羞、不大方的

I'm a little shy around new faces... It might be really awkward.
我對新面孔會有點害羞…也許會很尷尬。

🖉get over: 克服

Bean

I hear ya. I was at first too but everyone is so nice you get over it real quick!
我知道了，我一開始也是這樣，但每個人都很親切，妳可以很快克服的！

天鵝

Ok then. I'll give it a try!
那麼好的，我會試試看！

Bean

Yay!!!
耶！！

 與新朋友見面有關的句子

I feel awkward in a room full of people I don't know. 在一個全是我不認識的人的房間裡，我會覺得尷尬。

How can I start a conversation at a party where I don't know anyone?
在一個沒有我認識的人的派對上，我要如何開始對話？

She can easily walk up to a stranger and start chatting. 她可以輕易走向陌生人聊天。

We've only met a few times but he feels like an old friend. 我們只見過幾次，但感覺他像個老朋友。

Meeting people in person that you've met online can be dangerous!
直接與網路上遇到的人見面會很危險！

That's my show!

那是我最喜歡的節目！

 安琪兒

*episode: 電視節目的 1 集

Did you see last night's episode of Queen of Beauty?
妳有看昨晚的 <Queen of Beauty> 嗎？

*show: 電視節目　　天鵝

U watch it too?! OMG That's my show!
妳也看了？ 喔！那是我最喜歡的節目！

 安琪兒

I don't think I can wait until next week's episode...
我等不及要看下禮拜的一集了⋯

*cliffhanger: 驚險刺激的狀況　　天鵝

Me neither. I hate cliffhangers like that.
我也是，我討厭那樣提心吊膽的。

 安琪兒

Yeah seriously. And when are they going to kiss already?!!?!?!
嗯，真的，而且他們何時才要接吻？

*drag out: 拖　　天鵝

I know, right!? How long are they going to drag this out?
沒錯，對吧？他們要拖到何時？

安琪兒

🎧 get a contract w/: get a contract with, 與 ~ 簽約

BTW, did you hear the actor that plays Haneul got a contract w/ 'M' Makeup?

順便一提，妳聽說飾演 Haneul 的演員與 "M" 化妝品公司簽約了嗎？

🎧 It's no surprise.: 當然 / stunning: 極迷人的

天鵝

It's no surprise. She is stunning after all.

這是當然的，畢竟她非常迷人。

安琪兒

I heard she's also appearing on a variety show Tuesday night.

我聽說她也出現在星期二晚上的綜藝節目。

🎧 be a huge fan of ~: 是 ~ 的狂熱粉絲

天鵝

I'll have to tune in. I'm a huge fan of hers.

我會鎖定頻道，我是她的狂粉。

與 TV 有關的句子

More to Talk!

Daytime soap operas are absolutely addictive! 晨間連續劇完全使人沉迷！

You ordered another item off the home shopping channel? 你又在購物頻道訂購了商品？

I am going to hurry home to try to catch tonight's game. 我要快點回家看今晚的比賽。

There are so many commercials for skin creams. 乳霜的廣告太多了。

Can you see what else is on? This is boring. 你能看其他的節目嗎？這個好無聊。

Just the thought of it makes me cringe. 光想就覺得難為情。

Tae

> My boss is irritated with me.
> 我老闆對我很生氣。

King_Michael

> What did you do now? Lol
> 你做了什麼？呵呵。

Tae

🖉 ur = you're

> I went home before my coworkers went to a singing room last night.
> 昨天晚上在同事們去 KTV 之前我回家了。

🖉 shoulda just gone: should have just gone   **King_Michael**

> You shoulda just gone.
> 你應該去的。

Tae

🖉 cringe: 畏縮的、難為情的

> And sing in front of everyone? Just the thought of it makes me cringe.
> 然後在每個人面前唱歌？光想就覺得難為情。

🖉 make an excuse: 找藉口   **King_Michael**

> It looks bad to be the first person to leave.
> Did u make a good excuse at least?
> 第一個離開的人觀感不好，你至少有找個好藉口吧？

Tae

I pretended to be drunk but everyone knows I really wasn't.
我假裝喝醉了，但每個人都知道我其實沒有。

✏get over one's fear: 克服恐懼 / b/4: before　　**King_Michael**

You're going to have to get over your fear
b/4 everyone at work hates u.
在每個同事討厭你之前，你必須克服你的恐懼。

Tae

✏sign up for ~: 報名

That's why I signed up for singing
lessons this morning.
那就是為什麼今天早上我報名了唱歌課。

King_Michael

Good thinking.
想得好。

 ## 與 KTV 有關的句子

You can order more beer if you like. 如果你喜歡，你可以點更多啤酒。

My boss usually wears his tie on his head when he has a few too many.
當我的老闆喝多時，他通常會把領帶繫在頭上。

If you can't sing, dance and play the tambourine instead! 如果你不會唱歌，
就用跳舞和拍鈴鼓代替！

There are lots of English songs to choose from. 有很多英文歌可以從中挑選。

Once you pick your song, enter the number like this. 一旦你選好了歌，像這
樣輸入號碼。

I hate when somebody ruins the fun atmosphere with some sappy
ballad. 我討厭有人唱一些傷感的抒情歌來破壞歡樂的氣氛。

I feel like an entirely new person.
我覺得好像煥然一新。

天鵝

> Hey, can you tell me the name of your yoga studio again?
> 嘿，你能再告訴我你的瑜珈教室名稱嗎？

Bean

> Lotus Yoga
> Lotus 瑜珈。

天鵝

> Ah, right. Thanks!
> 嗯，謝啦！

🎵facilities: 設施　　　　　　　　　Bean

> You're going to love it! Their teachers are so professional and the facilities are all brand new.
> 妳會喜歡的！他們的老師非常專業，設施是全新的。

天鵝

> Really?
> 真的？

Bean

> Yeah, they just renovated the whole building. It's fantastic.
> 嗯，他們剛整修了整棟大樓，非常棒。

天鵝

> Cool.
> 真酷。

Bean

> The prices aren't bad either. If you sign up for three months you get a 30% discount. I did a whole year and got a free mat and some other yoga gear.
> 價格也不錯，如果妳報名三個月會有 30% 的折扣，我報名了一年，得到了免費瑜珈墊和其他一些瑜珈用品。

天鵝

> Neat.
> 不錯呢。

Bean

Since starting I've lost 2 kilos, my skin has gotten clearer, and my back doesn't hurt anymore!
開始上課後我瘦了 2 公斤，我的皮膚變得更光滑，背部也不再痛了。

天鵝

That's great news.
那真是好消息。

Bean

I feel like an entirely new person! So which class are you going to take? A.M. Beginners?
我覺得好像煥然一新！那麼妳想上哪種課程呢？早上初級班？

天鵝

Oh I just needed the name for my GPS. I want to go to the bookstore next door but can't remember the name.
喔，我只是需要在 GPS 上面輸入名稱，我想要去隔壁的書店，但不記得名稱。

Bean

Oh... Lol :P
啊…呵呵呵。

與團報、報名有關的句子

They offer a one month free trial for new members. 他們為新會員提供一個月免費體驗。

I registered for flower arranging classes at the florist down the street.
我報名了街上花店的插花課程。

Their hiking club goes to a different mountain every other Saturday.
他們的登山俱樂部每個隔週的星期六都去不同的山。

If you can't meet up in person then try joining an online community.
如果你不能直接見面，那就試著加入網路社群。

A book club seems like a great way to think more deeply about important issues. 要對重要議題有更深入的思考，讀書俱樂部似乎是個好方法。

Where is your sense of adventure? 你的冒險心到哪裡去了？

Tae

Any interest in going to Jeju this summer vacation?
這次暑假有興趣去濟州嗎？

way behind: 落後的　　King_Michael

I don't know... I'm way behind on my studies.
我不知道⋯我的功課落後太多。

Tae

Ur:You're / pass up: 放棄、拒絕

Seriously?
Ur gonna pass up this trip to go to some academy again?
你是說真的？你又放棄這次旅行去什麼補習班嗎？

Tae

Think about the girls!
想想看女孩們！

King_Michael

What girls? You guys are gonna be surfing the whole time...
什麼女孩？你們整天都在衝浪而已⋯

Tae

BBQ; 烤肉

Not the WHOLE time.
We'll be BBQing and drinking after sunset ;)
不是「整天」，天黑後我們會烤肉和喝酒。

tempting. 誘惑的、吸引人的　King_Michael

> Hmm...it's tempting but...
> 嗯…很吸引人…但是…

Tae

> But what?
> 但是什麼？

beef up: 強化、加強　King_Michael

> I've got to beef up my resume before I graduate.
> 在畢業之前我必須加強我的履歷表。

Tae 　sense of adventure: 冒險心 / refresh: 充電

> Bro, where is your sense of adventure? Sand, sun, sea... girls. You need to refresh before next semester.
> 兄弟，你的冒險心到哪裡去了？細沙、陽光、大海…女孩們。你需要在下學期來臨之前充個電。

count ~ in: 算我一個　King_Michael

> Yeah... alright. Count me in.
> 好吧…算我一個。

 與謝絕好意有關的句子

Well, the thing is… I've already made other plans. 其實…我已經有其他計畫了。

I want to, but I'm afraid I can't. 我想要，但是我怕我不能。

It seems like a good idea, but I don't think it'll work. 這似乎是個好主意，但我不覺得能成功。

I want to... but I really can't. 我想要…但我真的不行。

I see what you're saying but I'll have to disagree. 我知道你要說什麼，但我無法同意。

ChitChat 076　　　　　　　　p 188

Bored out of my mind.

(I'm) Bored out of my mind. 無聊死了。
sit in 只待在家
Wanna? 要嗎？
ride a bike 騎腳踏車
kite 風箏
fly a kite 放風箏
gather 聚集
sand castle 沙堡
tan 曬黑
ballpark 棒球場
Cherry Blossom Festival 櫻花慶典
go on a double date 兩對一起約會

ChitChat 077　　　　　　　　p 190

I haven't gone anywhere in ages.

I can't afford it. 我沒有那種閒暇時間。
sis(sister) 姊妹
homemaking 家事
work 24/7 不分日夜地工作
It's bad timing. 時機不好。
Maybe some other time. 也許下次有機會。
You tell me. 可不是？
I haven't gone anywhere in ages. 我好久沒去什麼地方了。
We'll see. 再看看。
See you in 20. 20 分鐘後見。
Can I take a rain check? 我可以留到下次嗎？
Don't be a stranger. 不要沒聯絡。

ChitChat 078　　　　　　　　p 192

He's an athletic freak.

talk nonsense 瞎扯淡
give advice 給予建議
well-informed 見多識廣的
athletic freak 運動狂
He's an athletic freak. 他是一個運動狂。
well-built 健壯的
Don't rub it in. 不要在傷口上撒鹽。
It's on me. 我請客。
treadmill 跑步機
run on the treadmill 在跑步機上跑步
footwear 鞋子
joint 關節
protect your joints 保護你的關節
workout routine 訓練內容
set up the workout routine 設定訓練內容
Stay hydrated. 保持水份。
6-pack abs 6 塊腹肌

ChitChat 079　　　　　　　　p 194

I'm drawn to baking classes.

certified barista 認證過的咖啡師
I have mixed feelings. 我的心情很複雜。
coffee place 咖啡店
expertise 專業知識
picture oneself 想像
I can't picture ~ 我不能想像 ~
run a bakery 經營麵包店
I'm drawn to baking classes. 我對烘培課有興趣。

at least 至少
temp 臨時性的
9-to-5ers 正職員工
quality time 寶貴的時光

ChitChat 080 p 196
Let's get together more often.

That was a blast. 太興奮了。
fat burning 脂肪燃燒
stress relief 消除壓力
killing two birds with one stone 一石二鳥
muscular 肌肉的
I know. 沒錯。
positive outlet 正面的發洩出口
fit and healthy 身體健康的
Hear! Hear! 說得好！說得好！
Hit the gym. 去健身房。
after work 下班後
calories 卡路里
metabolism 新陳代謝
strength training 肌力訓練

ChitChat 081 p 198
It was a waste of time.

a big fan of ~ ~ 的狂熱粉絲
cinema 電影院
kill the excitement 使失去趣味
waste of time 浪費時間
nap 小睡
take a nap 小睡一下
Who's it starring? 誰主演的？

ChitChat 082 p 200
No wonder you're so good at English!

convo conversation 的簡稱，對話
No wonder you're so good at English.
難怪妳的英文很好。
give it a shot 試一次看看
simultaneously 同時
be better off ~ 會更好
currently 現在
shy 害羞、不大方的
get over 克服

ChitChat 083 p 202
That's my show!

show 電視節目
That's my show. 那是我最喜歡的節目。
cliffhanger 驚險刺激的狀況
drag out 拖
get a contract with ~ 與 ~ 簽約
It's no surprise. 當然。
stunning 極迷人的
variety show 綜藝節目
soap opera 連續劇
addictive 使人沉迷的
commercial 電視廣告
What else is on? 你能看其他的節目嗎？

ChitChat 084 p 204

Just the thought of it makes me cringe.

irritated with ~ 對 ~ 惱怒
coworker 同事
singing room KTV
Just thought of it makes me cringe.
光想就覺得難為情。
cringe 畏縮的、難為情的
excuse 藉口
make an excuse 找藉口
pretend to be drunk 假裝喝醉
fear 恐懼
singing lessons 唱歌課
tambourine 鈴鼓
ruin the fun atmosphere 破壞氣氛
sappy 多愁善感的
ballad 抒情歌

ChitChat 085 p 206

I feel like an entirely new person.

yoga 瑜珈
professional 專業的
facilities 設施
brand new 全新的
renovate 整修
get a discount 得到折扣
yoga gear 瑜珈用品
Neat! 不錯！
lose 2 kilos 瘦了 2 公斤

I feel like an entirely new person. 我覺得好像煥然一新。
book store 書店
free trial 免費體驗
register for ~ 報名 ~
flower arranging classes 插花課程
florist 花店
every other Saturday 每個隔週的星期六
In person 直接

ChitChat 086 p 208

Where is your sense of adventure?

behind on one's studies 學業落後
pass up 放棄、拒絕
academy 補習班
BBQ 烤肉
after sunset 天黑後
tempting 誘惑的、吸引人的
beef up 強化、加強
Where is your sense of adventure?
你的冒險心到哪裡去了？
refresh 充電
semester 學期
Count me in. 算我一個。
make plans 制定計畫
disagree 不同意

CHAT

08

Everyday Life and Problems
日常生活與問題

What am I? Chopped liver?

我算啥？什麼也不是？

小秘書   🖊 bf: boy friend 的簡稱、男朋友

My new bf is smart, funny, and handsome... but...
我的新男友很聰明、有趣、英俊…，但

Jas

So?
然後？

小秘書   🖊 inconsistent: 反覆無常的 / absent-minded: 恍神的、健忘的

He's so inconsistent and absent-minded!
他很反覆無常又健忘。

Jas

I guess you can't have it all.
我想妳沒辦法擁有一切。

小秘書

He totally forgot my birthday today!
他完全忘了今天是我的生日！

🖊 BTW: by the way / b-day: birthday 的簡稱   Jas

Oh, BTW, happy b-day!
喔，順便祝妳生日快樂！

小秘書　✏️I don't care about you.: 我不在乎你。

Oh I don't care about you!
噢，你無所謂。

✏️chopped liver: 不重要的、無意義的人 (事物)　Jas

What am I? Chopped liver?
我算啥？什麼也不是？

小秘書

You know what I mean!
你知道我的意思！

　✏️Like I said.: 就像我說的　Jas

So kind. Like I said, you can't have it all.
妳很好，就像我說的，妳沒辦法擁有一切。

 與要求有關的句子

Is that too much to ask? 這是太過份的要求嗎？

That sounds too much to ask of him. 那聽起來是對他要求太多了。

Just name it. I'll get it for you. 儘管說，我就會給妳。

Do it! Would it kill you or what? 做！難道這個會殺了你還是什麼嗎？

Don't bite off more than you can chew. 量力而為。

More to Talk!

Cutting food waste helps us go greener. 減少廚餘有助我們成為環保者。

 安琪兒

R u using food trash bags too?
你也在使用廚餘垃圾袋嗎？

 Jas

What?
什麼？

 安琪兒

Food trash bags.
廚餘垃圾袋。

 Jas

🖉nah: no 的口語

Nah. I separate the other trash though.
不，不過我有做其他的垃圾分類。

 安琪兒

🖉disposable (plastic) bags: 專用垃圾袋 / convenience store: 便利商店

You're supposed to bag your food waste.
They sell disposable bags at convenience stores.
你應該把廚餘裝在袋子裡，便利商店有賣專用垃圾袋。

 Jas

🖉I C: I see 的網路簡寫

I C. It's a practical way to help reduce the amount of food garbage.
原來如此，這是減少廚餘量的實用辦法。

安琪兒　　🎵Indeed: 的確

Indeed.
的確是。

🎵pay attention to ~: 對 ~ 關心　　Jas

I should pay more attention to that.
我應該更關心一點。

安琪兒

They say cutting food waste
helps us go greener.
據說減少廚餘可以使我們更環保。

Jas

Yeah, you should do your part as a citizen.
嗯，身為一個市民應該盡自己的責任。

More to Talk!

 ## 與環保有關的句子

Be sure to dry out your food waste before taking it out. 在丟棄廚餘之前要確認已乾燥處理。

Check your fridge and plan your meals before grocery shopping. 去商店購物之前要檢查你的冰箱和計畫菜單。

Don't scrape leftovers into the bin. Instead, use them as ingredients for the next meal. 不要把剩菜剩飯倒進垃圾桶，而是把它們當成下一餐的材料。

Make it a habit to freeze any leftover food. 養成冷凍剩餘食物的習慣。

Try to cook only as much as you can eat. 只煮你能吃完的份量。

She never throws anything away.

她從來不丟東西。

小秘書

> **U know June?**
> 妳知道 June 嗎？

roomie: 室友

Kell2013

> **Ur roomie?**
> 妳的室友？

小秘書　　odd: 古怪的、異常的

> **Yes. She's odd.**
> 對，她很奇怪。

Kell2013

> **How odd?**
> 怎麼奇怪？

小秘書　　　　　　throw away: 丟棄

> **She never throws anything away.**
> 她從來不丟東西。

Kell2013

> **Really?**
> 真的嗎？

小秘書　　　inaccessible: 難於接近的

> **Her room is overflowing with stuff n completely inaccessible.**
> 她的房間都是東西，完全進不去。

♪hoarder: 有強迫性囤積症的人、囤積癖　Kell2013

What a hoarder!
完全是個囤積癖！

小秘書

♪every single day: 每天每天

Plus more boxes come in every single day.
而且每天都多了一些箱子。

Kell2013

Sounds serious.
聽起來很嚴重。

小秘書

♪break down the wall: 拆牆

Someday I'll need to break down the wall to reach her.
總有一天我得拆牆才能靠近她。

♪gimme a break = give me a break: 怎麼會、不會吧　Kell2013

Haha. Gimme a break. It can't be that bad!
哈哈，怎麼會，有那麼糟嗎？

More to Talk!

 ## 與房子打掃、清潔有關的句子

His house is cluttered with comic books. 他的家被漫畫書堆得亂七八糟。

I've never seen such a neat and tidy person as him. 我沒看過像他那樣乾淨整齊的人。

Her place is squeaky clean. 她的家一塵不染。

I can't put up with a messy person like you. 我不能容忍像你那樣骯髒的人。

It's been 2 months since I moved, but I haven't started unpacking yet.
我搬家已經 2 個月了，但我還沒開始打開行李。

I got caught jaywalking.

我被抓到亂穿越馬路。

 Jas

> I got busted.
> 我被抓到了。

電玩宅

> Doing what?
> 你做了啥？

 Jas

🔗jaywalking: 亂穿越馬路

> I got caught jaywalking.
> 我被抓到亂穿越馬路。

🔗straight shooter: 坦白正直的人 　　電玩宅

> And here I thought you were a straight shooter.
> 我以為你是坦率正直的人。

 Jas

🔗have no choice: 沒有選擇餘地 / be in a rush: 匆忙的

> I had no choice. I was in a rush.
> 我沒有選擇，我那時很匆忙。

🔗pay a fine: 罰款　　電玩宅

> I guess you'll have to pay a fine?
> 我想你必須付罰款？

Jas

♪cut ~ some slack: 給 ~ 網開一面

The police officer cut me some slack.
警察放我一馬。

電玩宅

Meaning what?
什麼意思？

Jas

♪warning: 警告

He let me go with a warning this time. :)
他說這次給我個警告。

電玩宅

Well aren't you lucky!!!
你真幸運！！

 ## 與違反交通有關的句子

He ran the red light. 他闖紅燈了。

The police gave him a speeding ticket. 警察給他開了超速的罰單。

She slammed on the brakes not to hit the pedestrian.
她緊急剎車以免撞到行人。

He's a victim of a hit and run. 他是肇事逃逸的被害者。

I had to pay a fine for illegal parking. 我必須繳交違規停車的罰款。

Just for kicks.

只是為了好玩。

Kell2013

🎧 reunion: 同學會

Did I tell you I was at the high school reunion yesterday?
我告訴妳昨天我去高中同學會了嗎？

安琪兒

Wow. It's not like U.
哇～這不像妳。

Kell2013 🎧 for kicks: 為了好玩

I know. Just for kicks.
我知道，只是為了好玩。

🎧 What did I miss?: 我錯過了什麼嗎？ 安琪兒

So, what did I miss?
所以我錯過了什麼嗎？

Kell2013 🎧 squeaky: 嘎嘎作響、發出刺耳聲的

Remember Eugene with the high squeaky voice?
記得那個聲音很刺耳的 Eugene 嗎？

安琪兒

Sure do.
當然。

Kell2013 🎧 remarry: 再婚

He remarried his ex-wife.
他與前妻又結婚了。

安琪兒

Wow. That is new.
哇，那真是新鮮。

Kell2013

And Young's expecting his third baby.
Young 的第三個孩子快出生了。

安琪兒

Attaboy!!!
做得好！！

Kell2013

Haha.
哈哈。

juicy: 有趣的、多汁的　安琪兒

Any other juicy stories?
還有其他有趣的嗎？

Kell2013 　　sweetheart: 戀人

Like the one about ur high school sweetheart?
像妳高中時交往的戀人這樣的？

Who cares!: 誰在乎！　　安琪兒

Whoa! He chose Yoori over me. Who cares?
夠了！他選了 Yoori 而不是我，誰在乎？

 與結婚有關的句子

My ex invited me to his engagement party. 我前男友邀請我去他的訂婚典禮。

They are known for splitting up. 大家都知道他們分居了。

Where's the wedding reception? 婚宴在哪裡？

He decided to remarry for his son. 他決定為了兒子再婚。

Marriages of convenience are nothing new. 基於利益的婚姻不是什麼新鮮事了。

I'm already regretting it.

我已經後悔了。

安琪兒

Ask me who I saw today.
問我今天看到誰了。

Kell2013

Who?
誰？

安琪兒

Chan from Boy's Generation!!
少年時代的 Chan！

Kell2013

Oh, was he cute?
噢，他可愛嗎？

安琪兒

♪ star-struck:（對藝人）完全沉迷的

I got star-struck! I almost walked into a pole.
我完全沉迷了！我差點就撞到柱子。

Kell2013

lol
呵呵

安琪兒

He he
嘿嘿

autograph: 簽名 Kell2013

Get an autograph?
拿到簽名了嗎？

安琪兒 *Nope: No 的口語說法*

Nope!
沒有！

Kell2013

Why not?
為什麼？

安琪兒 *tacky: 俗氣的、寒酸的 / celeb: celebrity 的簡寫*

It's tacky to ask a celeb for an autograph.
向明星要求簽名很俗氣。

once-in-a-lifetime chance: 千載難逢的機會 Kell2013

Could have been your once-in-a-lifetime chance to meet him, though.
不過這可能是妳千載難逢的機會。

安琪兒 *regret: 後悔*

Actually, I'm already regretting it.
其實我已經後悔了。

與機率、機會有關的句子

Not a chance. 門兒都沒有。
Why not take a chance? 為何不碰碰運氣？
You have no chance of getting her back. 你沒有勝算讓她回心轉意。
I'll take a chance on that. 我會嘗試一次。
Luckily enough, I got a second chance. 很幸運地我有了第二次機會。

It's like the 7th solid day of rain. 好像下了七天份的雨。

 天鵝

I'm bored!!!
我好無聊！！

🎙~ or something: ~ 之類的

Bean

Do some shopping or something.
可以去購物之類的。

 天鵝

I am already. Hehe.
我已經在購物了，嘿嘿。

Bean

Where at?
在哪裡？

 天鵝

We-Dome.
We-Dome。

Bean

Wish I were there with you.
真希望我能和妳在那裡。

 天鵝   🎙likewise: 一樣的、我也是

Likewise.
我也是。

🎙drizzling: 下毛毛雨   Bean

Uhh, looks like it's drizzling out.
嗯，外面看起來在下毛毛雨。

天鵝

Not here... Oh, no!!!
這裡沒有…噢，不！！

Bean

What's wrong?
怎麼了？

天鵝   🔖 pouring: 下傾盆大雨

It started pouring.
開始下大雨了。

🔖 clear up: 雨停、晴朗   Bean

Wait inside there until it clears up.
在裡面等到雨停。

天鵝

Yeah. It's like the 7th sold day of rain. :'(
嗯，好像下了七天份的雨。

🔖 sick of ~: 厭倦的、受夠 ~   Bean

I know! I'm sick of it!!!
我知道，真是受夠了！！

More to Talk!

 與下雨有關的句子

It's raining cats and dogs. 下傾盆大雨

I stepped in a puddle and now my shoes are all wet. 我踩到水坑，現在我的鞋子全都濕了。

The rainy season seems especially long this year. 今年的雨季似乎特別長。

I feel like eating bindaetteok and Makkoli whenever it rains. 下雨時我就想吃綠豆煎餅和韓國米酒。

I was caught in heavy rain. 我被暴雨困住了。

I don't mind walking in light rain. 我不介意淋點小雨。

Maybe he has some other issue. 也許牠有一些其他的問題。

 安琪兒

Vic is such a pain.
Vic 令人頭痛。

Kell2013

What did he do this time?
這次牠做了什麼？

 安琪兒

He just pooped on my rug.
牠剛剛在我的地毯上大便。

Kell2013

Oh, no. That was really pricey too...
喔，不，而且那是很貴的…

 安琪兒

I've done everything I can.
我已經盡力了。

✍ potty training: 大便訓練　　　　　Kell2013

He has no problem other than the potty training.
牠除了大便訓練以外都沒問題。

 安琪兒

True. But that's driving me crazy.
沒錯，但那讓我快瘋了。

Kell2013

Maybe he has some other issue.
也許牠有一些其他的問題。

安琪兒

Know any reliable obedience school?
知道哪裡有值得信任的寵物訓練所嗎？

Kell2013

Let me ask around.
讓我問問看。

安琪兒

I should do something before it's too late.
我必須先做點什麼以免為時已晚。

Kell2013

Good thinking.
好主意。

More to Talk!

與寵物有關的句子

I usually walk my puppy every day for about half an hour. 我通常每天遛狗 30 分鐘。

R U a cat person or a dog person? 你喜歡貓還是狗？

He recently adopted an abandoned dog. 他最近領養了流浪狗。

Pets come with big responsibilities. 寵物伴隨著很大的責任。

He uses his cute puppy to pick up girls. 他利用他可愛的小狗來勾引女生。

Guys, bundle up.
大家多穿一點。

 小秘書

🔖freezing cold: 非常寒冷

I heard it's freezing cold outside.
我聽說外面非常冷。

安琪兒

Yeah. I heard that, too.
嗯，我也聽說了。

Kell2013

Let's go see a movie and then do some shopping.
去看場電影和買些東西吧！

 小秘書

Did you guys reserve tickets?
妳們預約電影票了嗎？

🔖matinee: 週間的表演　　安琪兒

Yeah, we booked a 4:30 matinee.
嗯，我們訂了 4 點 30 分的場次。

 Kell2013　　🔖grab a dinner: 吃晚餐

Then let's grab dinner after.
然後再去吃晚餐。

 小秘書

Great. Let's hang inside.
好，在室內玩吧！

🔖bundle up: 多穿一點　安琪兒

Bundle up, guys!
大家多穿一點！

小秘書

I'm not worried. We're gonna go to an indoor mall!
我不擔心，我們要去室內購物中心。

Kell2013

🔖nice and cozy: 非常舒適的

And the movie theater should be nice and cozy as well!
而且電影院也應該會很舒適！

小秘書

☺

安琪兒

Yayyyyy. Finally we're all hanging out!!!
耶 ~~~ 我們終於全部都出來玩了！

與室內活動有關的句子

Let's stay in until it clears up. 待在裡面直到放晴吧！

We're so different. He's a homebody and I like to go out. 我們很不一樣，他喜歡待在家裡，我喜歡出去。

I stayed cooped up inside all weekend but at least I finished my novel.
我整個週末都困在房裡，但至少我看完小說了。

I really want to minimize time spent doing housework. 我真的想要把花在家務的時間減到最少。

He started wearing that stupid belly fat burner belt all around the house.
他開始在家裡都戴著那個可笑的腹部脂肪燃燒帶。

Not in a million years.
絕對不會了。

 Kell2013

> **What happened?**
> 發生什麼事了？

安琪兒

> **I got into a little car accident.**
> 我發生了一點小車禍。

 Kell2013 　✏OMG: Oh, my god 的網路用語

> **OMG. Did you get hurt?**
> 我的天啊，妳受傷了嗎？

安琪兒
> **No.**
> 沒有。

 Kell2013

> **Thank goodness.**
> 太好了。

✏claim to be injured: 宣稱受傷了　　安琪兒
> **But the other driver claimed to be injured.**
> 但對方駕駛說他受傷了。

✏fender bender: 輕微車禍 / No biggie: No big deal 沒什麼　　安琪兒
> **It was just a fender bender. No biggie.**
> 這只是個輕微車禍，沒啥大不了的。

Kell2013

How did it happen?
這是怎麼發生的？

安琪兒

I had to swerve to avoid
hitting a stray dog.
我必須轉彎以避免撞到流浪狗。

Kell2013

Is it okay?
狗還好嗎？

安琪兒

Yes.
嗯。

Kell2013 ✏ a stroke of luck: 走運、天佑神助

It was a stroke of luck for him.
牠真是走運。

✏ Not in a million years: 絕對不會　　安琪兒

I'll never drive again!! Not in a million years!!!
我絕對不再開車了！！永遠都不會了！！

 與交通事故有關的句子

He junked his car after the car crash. 他在車禍之後把車子報廢了。

She was a victim of the head-on collision. 她是正面碰撞的受害者。

Your car insurance will cover the theft. 你的車險包含了竊盜險。

See if your auto insurance will cover the flood damage. 看看你的車險是否包含了泡水受損。

I had to pay 40% of the bill after the car accident. 車禍之後我必須付 40% 的費用。

I had my fortune told.

我去算命了。

Kell2013 🔖have one's fortune told: 算命

I had my fortune told.
我去算命了。

Jas

What for?
算什麼？

Kell2013

I feel uneasy about the future.
我對未來感到不安。

🔖on a roll: 運勢正好 **Jas**

No need. You're on a roll now.
不需要，妳現在運勢正好。

Kell2013 🔖job insecurity: 工作不穩定 / haunt: 縈繞在心頭、無法停止思考

This job insecurity haunts me.
我總是覺得這個工作不穩定。

Jas

But you hate being a regular worker.
但是妳討厭當一般員工。

Kell2013

> I know. That's why I choose this but...
> 我知道，那就是為何我選擇這個的原因，但是⋯

Jas

> You're gonna be all right.
> 妳會順利的。

Kell2013

> For sure?
> 真的嗎？

Jas

> 100 percent sure.
> 100% 確定。

More to Talk!

💡 與確信有關的句子

I'm sure he'll make it. 我確定他會成功的。

It is crystal clear that she's not into me. 很明顯她不喜歡我。

The final decision is still up in the air. 最後的決定還沒下來。

I'm not 100% positive about this. 我對這件事沒有 100% 的信心。

I bet he's going to pass the bar exam. 我打賭他會通過律師考試。

It cost me an arm and a leg. 錢包大失血。

天鵝

> Noooooooooo!!!
> 不！！

小秘書

> What? What?
> 什麼？什麼？

 broken: 故障的

天鵝

> I bought this 3 days ago and it's already broken.
> 我 3 天前買了這個，但已經壞掉了。

小秘書

> What's "THIS"?
> 「這個」是什麼？

天鵝　on a 12-month (installment) plan: 12 個月分期付款

> An RB watch I got on a 12-month installment plan!!!
> 我用 12 個月分期付款買了 RB 手錶。

小秘書

> Exchange it or get a refund.
> 換貨或退錢。

天鵝

But this was specially ordered and non-returnable.
但這個是特別訂購的，不能退貨。

小秘書

Well, then...
嗯…那麼…

天鵝

🖊 cost ~ an arm and a leg: 錢包大失血、浪費

It cost me an arm and a leg.
我錢包大失血了。

小秘書

Get it fixed or something.
去修理之類的。

天鵝

Arrggh. I'm never gonna waste my money again on this stupid kind of thing.
啊…我絕對不要再把錢浪費在這個笨東西上了。

More to Talk!

💡 與價錢有關的句子

It cost me a fortune. 我花了很多錢。

That was a steal. 那跟免費的沒兩樣。

That store charged me double the price. I got ripped off. 那家店收我兩倍價錢，我被削了。

The shop offers reasonable prices. 這家店的價錢很合理。

She's a super haggler.

她是討價還價的天才。

Kell2013

🎵the other day: 幾天前

I went to Dongdaemun the other day.
幾天前我去東大門。

🎵Any luck?: (不期待的) 有什麼收穫嗎？　小秘書

Any luck?
有什麼收穫嗎？

Kell2013

We got a good bargain.
我們買得很便宜。

小秘書

We?
我們？

Kell2013

瓊絲 and me.
瓊絲和我。

🎵haggler: 會講價的人　小秘書

I heard she's a super haggler.
我聽說她很會殺價。

Kell2013

The rumors are true!
傳聞是真的！

📌 have an eye for ~: 有眼光、會鑑別

小秘書

But does she have an eye for clothing?
不過她也有看衣服的眼光？

 Kell2013　　📌 I'll say: 我就說 / *BFF = best friend forever, BF = boyfriend, or best friend

I'll say. She's like a shopper's BFF.
我就說嘛，她是購物時的超級好朋友。

小秘書

You must feel lucky.
妳一定覺得很幸運。

 Kell2013

Anyway, I'm ready for spring!
不管怎樣我已經準備好迎接春天了！

小秘書

Great.
真棒。

More to Talk!

 與購物有關的句子

I'm going on a shopping spree. 我正在瘋狂購物。

I shop when I'm bored. 我無聊時就購物。

She sure is a smart shopper. 她明顯是個聰明購物者。

I normally browse several times before I buy anything. 我通常在買東西之前會看好幾次。

I prefer home shopping because they have a lenient return policy.
我喜歡在家購物，因為他們的退貨制度很寬鬆。

I'll have to eat and run.

我必須吃完就走。

Kell2013

> I'm in front of the station. Where r u all?
> 我在車站前面，妳在哪裡？

天鵝

> On my way!
> 在路上！

Bean

> Me 2. Be there in 5!
> 我也是，5 分鐘內到。

安琪兒

> Hope you guys don't mind but I'm bringing my husband!
> 希望妳們不介意，我帶先生來！

Tae
🖊 No prob.: No problem. 的簡寫，沒問題，沒關係 / w/o: without 的簡寫

> No prob! I'll be about 30 min late tho. Start w/o me!
> 沒關係！我會晚 30 分鐘到，妳們先開始！

Bean

> Tae, we knew that already. Ur late all the time! Lol
> Tae，我們都知道，你成天遲到！呵呵

Tae

> :p
> （吐舌）

電玩宅

Where's the restaurant again??
再問一次餐廳在哪裡？

King_Michael

🎵 heat exhaustion: 中暑

I'm here. Just looking for a place to park.
我到了，正在找停車位。

🎵 tho: though 的簡寫 / Sry.: Sorry. 的簡寫   Jas

Alllllllmost there. I'll have to eat and run tho. Sry guys!
快 ~~ 到了。我必須吃完就走，抱歉了，大家！

電玩宅

Found it! Thanks everyone for asking me to be part of your wine tasting group.
找到了！謝謝你們邀我成為你們的品酒同好會的一員。

🎵 on the move: 忙碌的   小秘書

Always on the move, Jas!
你總是很忙，Jas！

小秘書

Glad u can join our meetings. ☺
很高興你能參加我們的聚會。

More to Talk!

 與聚會有關的句子

I'm running a bit behind. 我會晚一點。
Will your girlfriend be able to join? 你的女友也能參加嗎？
My roommate can't come out tonight. 我的室友晚上不能來。
Could we change the meeting place? 我們能換一個見面地點嗎？
Let's meet at the coffee shop across the street. 在對街的咖啡店見面吧！
The best way to get there is by taxi. 到那裡最好的方法就是搭計程車。

ChitChat 087   p 214
What am I? Chopped liver?

inconsistent 反覆無常的
absent-minded 恍神的、健忘的
You can't have it all. 不能擁有全部。
chopped liver 不重要的人（事物）
like I said 就像我說的
Just name it. 儘管說。
Don't bite off more than you can chew. 量力而為。

ChitChat 088   p 216
Cutting food waste helps us go greener

trash bag 垃圾袋
separate 分離
bag 裝進袋子
convenience store 便利商店
reduce 減少
indeed 的確
do one's part 盡到～的責任
citizen 市民
take out 拿出去
fridge 冰箱
leftover 剩菜剩飯
ingredient 材料
make it habit to～ 養成～的習慣

ChitChat 089   p 218
She never throws anything away.

roomie(roommate) 室友
She never throws anything away. 她從來不丟東西。
overflow 溢出
hoarder 有強迫性囤積症的人、囤積癖
every single day 每天
break down 毀壞
Gimmie(give me) a break. 怎麼會、不會吧。
cluttered with～ 被～弄得亂七八糟
neat and tidy 乾淨整齊的
squeaky clean 一塵不染
put up with 忍受

ChitChat 090   p 220
I got caught jaywalking.

get busted 被抓到了
jaywalking 亂穿越馬路
I got caught jaywalking. 我被抓到亂穿越馬路。
straight shooter 正直坦率的人
pay a fine 交罰款
cut some slack 對～網開一面
warning 警告

ChitChat 091 p 222
Just for kicks.

reunion 同學會
just for kicks 為了好玩
What did I miss? 我錯過了什麼？
ex 前男友、前夫
expect a baby 孩子即將出生
Attaboy! 做得好！
juicy 有趣的
sweetheart 戀人
choose A over B 選擇 A 而不是 B

ChitChat 092 p 224
I'm already regretting it.

get star-struck（對藝人）完全沉迷的
get an autograph 拿到簽名
tacky 俗氣的、寒酸的
celeb celebrity 的簡寫，名人
once-in-a-lifetime chance 千載難逢的機會
I'm already regretting it. 我已經後悔了。
Not a chance. 門兒都沒有。

ChitChat 093 p 226
It's like the 7th solid day of rain.

drizzling 下毛毛雨
pouring 下傾盆大雨

clear up 雨停、晴朗
It's like the 7th solid day of rain. 好像下了七天份的雨。
It's raining cats and dogs. 下傾盆大雨
puddle 水坑
rainy season 雨季
heavy rain 暴雨

ChitChat 094 p 228
Maybe he has some other issue.

rug 地毯
pricey 昂貴的
potty training 大便訓練
issue 問題
Maybe he has some other issue. 也許牠有一些其他的問題。
ask around 問問看

ChitChat 095 p 230
Guys, bundle up.

freezing cold 非常寒冷的
grab dinner 吃晚餐
Bundle up, guys! 大家多穿一點！
cozy 舒適的
hang out 出去玩
housework 家事

ChitChat 096   p 232
Not in a million years.

get hurt 受傷
Thank goodness. 太好了。
fender bender 輕微車禍
No biggie. 沒什麼。
stray dog 流浪狗
a stroke of luck 走運
Not in a million years. 絕對不會了。
car crash 車禍
head-on collision 正面對撞車禍
auto insurance 車險

ChitChat 097   p 234
I had a fortune told.

I had my fortune told. 我去算命了。
uneasy 不安的
No need. 不需要。
on a roll 運勢正好
job insecurity 工作不穩定
haunt 無法停止思考
regular worker 一般員工
bar exam 律師考試

ChitChat 098   p 236
It cost me an arm and a leg.

broken 故障
installment plan 分期付款
non-returnable 不可退貨的

It cost me an arm and a leg. 錢包大失血。
fix 修理
That was a steal. 那跟免費的沒兩樣。
I got ripped off. 我被當凱子削了。
reasonable 合理的

ChitChat 099   p 238
She's a super haggler.

Any luck? 有什麼收穫嗎？
get a good bargain 買得很便宜
She's a super haggler. 她很會殺價。
I'll say. 我就說嘛。
shopper's BFF 購物時的超級好朋友
lenient 寬鬆

ChitChat 100   p 240
I'll have to eat and run.

(I'm) on my way. （我）在路上。
all the time 總是
I'll have to eat and run. 我必須吃完就走。
wine tasting 品酒
on the move 忙碌的
run behind 遲到

用 LINE、FB、IG 聊出好英文：只要 100 個日常小話題，英語能力大跳級！

作　　者：宋允貞 / Crystal L. Hecht
譯　　者：陳盈之
企劃編輯：王建賀
文字編輯：王雅雯
設計裝幀：張寶莉
發 行 人：廖文良

發 行 所：碁峰資訊股份有限公司
地　　址：台北市南港區三重路 66 號 7 樓之 6
電　　話：(02)2788-2408
傳　　真：(02)8192-4433
網　　站：www.gotop.com.tw
書　　號：ALE003500
版　　次：2020 年 05 月初版
建議售價：NT$320

國家圖書館出版品預行編目資料

用 LINE、FB、IG 聊出好英文：只要 100 個日常小話題，英語能力大跳級！/ 宋允貞, Crystal L. Hecht 原著；陳盈之譯. -- 初版. -- 臺北市：碁峰資訊, 2020.05
　　面；　公分
　　ISBN 978-986-502-477-2(平裝)
　　1.英語　2.會話
805.188　　　　31-1090513-7/5　　　　109005033

讀者服務

- 感謝您購買碁峰圖書，如果您對本書的內容或表達上有不清楚的地方或其他建議，請至碁峰網站：「聯絡我們」\「圖書問題」留下您所購買之書籍及問題。（請註明購買書籍之書號及書名，以及問題頁數，以便能儘快為您處理）
  http://www.gotop.com.tw

- 售後服務僅限書籍本身內容，若是軟、硬體問題，請您直接與軟、硬體廠商聯絡。

- 若於購買書籍後發現有破損、缺頁、裝訂錯誤之問題，請直接將書寄回更換，並註明您的姓名、連絡電話及地址，將有專人與您連絡補寄商品。